# ESSENTIAL
# PHYSICS

### Philippa Wingate

Illustrated by Sean Wilkinson and
Robert Walster

Designed by Robert Walster
Additional designs by John Russell and Radhi Parekh

Consultants: John Allen, Dr. Tom Petersen
and Paul Bonell
Series editor: Jane Chisholm

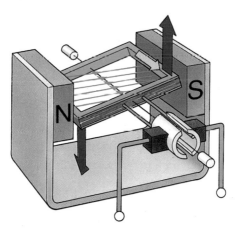

# Contents

# Using this book

*Essential Physics* is a concise reference book and revision aid. It is intended to act as a companion to your studies, explaining the essential points of physics clearly and simply.

Physics is the study of matter and energy, and the way in which matter and energy interact in the world around us. The book is divided into sections which cover the main concepts of physics. Each

section includes the key principles and facts for that topic, and their applications. Particularly important new words and equations are highlighted in **bold** type. If a word is explained in more detail on another page, it is printed in italic type with an asterisk, like this: *magnetism\**. At the foot of the page there is a reference to the page on which the explanation can be found.

## The information at the back of this book

The social, economic and environmental implications of some of the topics covered in the main part of the book are looked at in more detail in the black and white section at the back. This is followed by a variety of information, including a list of symbols used to represent components in electrical circuits, advice on number notation and constructing graphs.

You will also find a section which contains some of the more difficult mathematical ideas in physics. This includes some sample examination questions and model answers, to help you become familiar with using equations and mathematical ideas.

Finally, there is a glossary that explains difficult words in the text, and an index.

## Examinations

This book contains the essential information you will need when studying physics. For examinations, however, it is important to know which syllabus you are studying, because different examining

bodies require you to learn different material. You may find that there are topics in this book that you do not need to learn, or that certain topics covered by your syllabus do not appear in this book.

## Equations and symbols

When studying physics it is necessary to measure certain physical quantities, such as speed, weight and distance. Each of these quantities is given its own **symbol** and **unit** of measurement. For example, time is represented by the symbol t, and is measured in seconds (s).

To find some quantities, you have to multiply or divide others. The relationship between quantities can be expressed as an **equation**, either with words or symbols. For example, the relationship between force, mass and acceleration can be expressed as:

Force = mass x acceleration or F = ma.

In this book you will find triangles beside some of the equations in the text. These triangles are a mathematical device to help you remember and rearrange equations to find unknown quantities. The triangles contain the symbols of the quantities involved in the equations.

The triangles are used as follows:

Decide which quantity you wish to calculate. Cover up the symbol for that quantity.

If the symbol you have covered is at the bottom of the triangle, you will need to divide the quantity at the top of the triangle by the one which remains uncovered at the bottom.

If the symbol you have covered is at the top of the triangle, the two quantities at the bottom must be multiplied.

For example, in an examination question you might be asked to calculate the acceleration of a mass of 2 kg, when affected by a force of 6 newtons. Cover a, and replace the symbols for force and mass with their values.

$$a = \frac{6}{2} = 3 \text{ m/s}^2$$

# Structure and measurement of matter

All matter is made up of molecules. The smallest naturally occurring particle of any substance is called a **molecule**. Molecules are too small to be seen with the human eye, but their existence can be demonstrated by Brownian motion and diffusion, as described below.

Matter can exist in three physical states - as a **solid**, a **liquid** or a **gas**. The **kinetic theory** explains the structure and behaviour of substances in these states in terms of the motion of their molecules.

## Solids

The molecules in a solid are packed closely together in regular structures. They do not have enough energy to break free of the forces of attraction which bind them to their neighbouring molecules. They can only vibrate. This is why solids have a fixed shape and a fixed *volume*\* and do not flow like liquids.

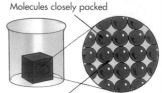

Molecules closely packed

Molecules can only vibrate.

## Liquids

Molecules have just enough energy to move.

The molecules in a liquid have just enough energy to break free of the forces which bind them to their neighbours. This is why liquids are able to flow and do not have a fixed shape. However, the forces are strong enough to hold the molecules close together, giving liquids a fixed volume.

## Gases

The molecules in a gas have so much energy that the force of attraction between them is negligible. They can move freely and at great speed. The molecules in a gas are much further apart than those in a liquid or a solid. This is why gases can be compressed easily.

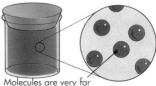

Molecules are very far apart, moving freely.

## Brownian motion

A cell of pollen grains in water

Microscope

Erratic path of pollen grains

The molecules in liquids and gases are continually moving in a completely random fashion. This is known as **Brownian motion**, after the botanist Sir Robert Brown who first studied the nature of their movement. He demonstrated that pollen grains placed in water move erratically. He decided this motion must be due to their unseen impact with water molecules. The tiny water molecules are able to move the much larger pollen grains because there is a large number of water molecules and they are moving very fast.

## Diffusion

**Diffusion** is the gradual mixing of two or more different gases or liquids. Diffusion happens when the molecules of the substances collide and intermingle. For example, the scent of flowers spreads through a room because its molecules diffuse through the air. The process of diffusion supports the idea that gases are made up of moving molecules, since the particles must be moving in order to mix.

## Atoms

Molecules are made up of groups of smaller particles called **atoms**. Atoms are formed of even smaller particles called **electrons**, **protons** and **neutrons**. The structure of an atom is shown here using the example of a helium atom. The central nucleus of an atom is formed of protons and neutrons. Protons have a positive *electrical charge*\* and neutrons have no charge. Protons and neutrons are approximately 2,000 times more massive than the electrons which orbit the nucleus. Electrons have a negative charge, equal in magnitude to the positive charge of the protons. The number of electrons in an atom is the same as the number of protons in the nucleus.

The number of protons in a nucleus is

*A helium atom*

The nucleus is a cluster of protons and neutrons.

The electrons are held in a 'cloud-like' orbit, attracted by the positive charge of the protons.

called the **proton number (Z)**. The total number of protons and neutrons in a nucleus is called the **nucleon number (A)**. The nucleon and the proton number of an atom are written next to the symbol for the *element*\* to which the atom belongs. For example, helium is written: $_2^4$He

## Measuring mass

The **mass** of an object is the measure of how much matter it contains. Mass is measured in **kilograms** (kg). To find the mass of an object, simple balancing scales like the ones shown are used to compare the unknown mass with a known mass.

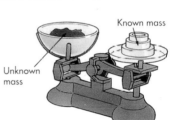

Known mass

Unknown mass

## Measuring volume

A Eureka can is filled with water.

The object displaces water into the measuring cylinder.

The object's volume is equal to the volume of the water it displaces.

The **volume** of an object is the measurement of the amount of space it occupies. It is measured in **cubic metres (m³)** or **cubic centimetres (cm³)**. The volume of regular shaped solids is found using a ruler and mathematical formulae. For example, the volume of a rectangular block is found using the equation: length x breadth x height. The volume of a liquid can be found by pouring it into a measuring cylinder. The volume of an irregular shaped solid is measured by **displacement** as shown in the diagram.

## Measuring density

Objects which are the same size and shape can vary greatly in mass. For example, one cubic centimetre of cork is much lighter than a cubic centimetre of lead. This is because the materials have a different **density**. Molecules of lead are heavier and more closely packed together than those of cork. This makes lead a more dense material than cork.

To find the density of a solid or a liquid its mass and volume must be measured using the methods described above. These quantities are used in the equation:

$$\text{Density (d)} = \frac{\text{mass (m)}}{\text{volume (v)}}$$

Density is measured in **kilograms per cubic metre (kg/m³)**, or **grammes per cubic centimetre (g/cm³)**.

---

\*Electrical charge, 31; Element, 61.

# Forces

A **force** is a push or a pull which can affect the motion of an object by changing its speed or direction. If two equal and opposite forces act on an object it may be squashed or stretched. Both the magnitude and direction of a force acting on an object must be stated, because both affect the way in which the object moves. If the direction in which a force is acting is known, it is possible to predict the way the object it affects may move. Forces are represented by arrowed lines whose length corresponds to the magnitude of the force. The arrow indicates the direction in which it is acting. Force is measured in **newtons (N)**.

A man pushing a broom with 2 N force.

A man exerting a stretching force of 40 N.

The golf club exerts a 50 N force.

A man exerting a 500 N pulling force.

## Magnetic and electrical forces

Magnets can exert a force of attraction and repulsion.

There are two types of forces which act at a distance: *magnetic** and *electrical** forces. Both types of force are described in detail later in the book. Objects which exert a magnetic or an electrical force can attract or repel objects which are brought near them. The region in which the forces act is called a **field**. The magnitude of the forces depends on the distance between the objects. The closer they are together, the stronger the force they exert.

## Gravitation and weight

**Gravitation** is another force which acts at a distance. It is the force which exists between any two masses, attracting them toward each other. Usually it is a weak force, but if one object is massive, such as a planet, the force becomes noticeable. Gravitational force depends

A man of mass 100 kg weighs 980 N on Earth. At a distance of 10,000 km from the Earth's surface, for example, he weighs only 150 N.

## Frictional forces

**Friction** is the force which resists the motion of two materials rubbing together. Sometimes it is a useful force - for example, it enables us to grip the ground as we walk. A vehicle is able to grip the road due to the friction between its tyres and the road surface. But friction also has unwanted effects. The friction between the moving parts of a *machine** produces heat which wastes energy. The friction between a cyclist and the air resists his or her forward movement.

Friction between the air and the cyclist's body

Friction between the tyres and the road

on the distance between objects. The closer the objects are together, the stronger the force they exert on each other.

**Weight** is a measure of a planet's gravitational pull on an object. Like all forces, it is measured in newtons (N). The weight of an object depends on its distance from a planet and the planet's mass. On the Earth's surface, the force of gravity acting on a mass of 1 kg is approximately 9.8 N. The magnitude of the force diminishes as the mass moves further away from the Earth's surface. An object's mass, however, remains the same wherever it is in the Universe.

6

*Magnetic forces, 36; Electrical forces, 31; Machine, 15.

## Elasticity

When a force is applied to an object which cannot move, the object stretches. Its molecules are pulled slightly apart and it becomes distorted. If the object remains distorted when the force is removed, its distortion is called **plastic**. If its molecules return to their original position, the distortion is called **elastic**. **Elasticity** is, therefore, a material's ability to return to its original shape. To study the elasticity of a material, such as a strip of copper, rubber or nylon, weights of increasing size are suspended from the material. The amount by which the material is stretched is found by subtracting its original length from its extended length. The size of the force is then increased and the results are used to make a graph.

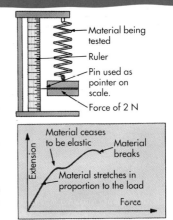

Material being tested

Ruler

Pin used as pointer on scale.

Force of 2 N

Material ceases to be elastic — Material breaks

Material stretches in proportion to the load

## Hooke's law

Hooke's law states that **the extension of a material is proportional to the force which is stretching it.**

There is a point, however, beyond which Hooke's law is no longer obeyed. This is called the **limit of proportionality.** If the substance is stretched further than this point, it reaches its **elastic limit.** The substance stops being elastic and remains distorted even when the stretching force is removed.

Provided a material's elastic limit is not exceeded, the principle of Hooke's law can be used in calculations to determine an unknown force or extension. For example, if a force of 10 N stretches a spring by 60 mm, the force which would produce an extension of 42 mm is calculated as follows:

60 mm extension is produced by 10 N

1 mm extension is produced by $\frac{10}{60}$

Therefore, the force which would produce a 42 mm extension is calculated as follows:

$$\frac{10 \times 42}{60} = 7 \, N$$

## A spring balance

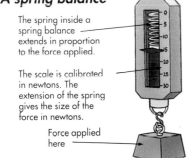

The spring inside a spring balance extends in proportion to the force applied.

The scale is calibrated in newtons. The extension of the spring gives the size of the force in newtons.

Force applied here

The easiest way of measuring forces is to use a **spring balance**, often called a **Newton balance.** This is a device containing a spring. The spring obeys Hooke's law. This means that it stretches in direct proportion to the force applied to it. For example, if the force applied to the spring is doubled, its extension doubles. The spring balance will measure forces accurately until it is stretched beyond its elastic limit and it becomes permanently distorted.

## Scalar and vector quantities

Quantities in physics are described as either scalar or vector quantities.

A **scalar** quantity is one which has magnitude only. For example, mass and temperature are scalar quantities.

A **vector** quantity is one which has both direction and magnitude. Force is a vector quantity. The magnitude and direction of a vector must always be stated. Vectors can be represented with arrowed lines.

# Turning forces

If an object is fixed at a point around which it may rotate, the point is called the **fulcrum**. If a force is applied to it, at a distance from the fulcrum, the object may rotate. This turning effect is called a

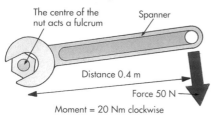

The centre of the nut acts a fulcrum

Spanner

Distance 0.4 m

Force 50 N

Moment = 20 Nm clockwise

**moment.** A moment is exerted if a door is opened, if a crowbar is used to lift a load and when a spanner turns a nut.

The moment which tries to rotate an object in a anticlockwise direction is called an **anticlockwise moment**. The moment which tries to turn the object clockwise is called a **clockwise moment**.

A turning moment is equal to the magnitude of the force, multiplied by the distance of the point where the force is acting from the fulcrum. This is written:

**Moment = force x distance from fulcrum.**
Turning moments are measured in **newton metres (Nm)**.

## The principle of moments

If an object is in **equilibrium** (or balanced), the sum of the clockwise moments about any point is equal to the sum of the anticlockwise moments about the same point. This is the principle of moments and, when two moments are exerted, this is written as follows:

**Weight$_1$ x distance$_1$ = Weight$_2$ x distance$_2$**

If an object is in equilibrium it is possible to calculate an unknown weight, or the unknown distance between a weight and the fulcrum. For example, the seesaw shown here is 2 m long. It is balanced. Child A weighs 200 N and sits 0.75 m

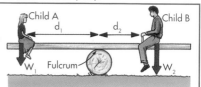

Child A
$d_1$
$d_2$
Child B
$W_1$ Fulcrum $W_2$

from the fulcrum, or point of balance. Child B, of unknown weight, sits 0.5 m from the fulcrum. The weight of child B can be calculated as follows:

$$W_1 \times d_1 = W_2 \times d_2$$
$$200 \times 0.75 = W_2 \times 0.5$$
$$W_2 = \frac{200 \times 0.75}{0.5}$$
$$W_2 = 300 \text{ N}$$

## The centre of gravity

An object's **centre of gravity** is the point through which its total weight is considered to act. The centre of gravity of a regular shaped object is its geometrical centre. For example, the centre of gravity of a square is the point at which lines bisecting each of its angles cross.

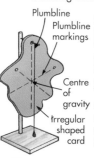

Plumbline

Plumbline markings

Centre of gravity

Irregular shaped card

The centre of gravity of an irregular shaped flat object is found by suspending it from a pin fixed in a clamp and hanging a plumbline from the pin. The position of the plumbline is marked. This is repeated with the pin at different places on the shape's edge. The centre of gravity lies where all the plumbline markings intersect.

## Stability

The **stability** of an object is its ability to return to its original position when tilted. Stability is governed by the position of an object's centre of gravity and the surface area of its base.

Stable objects have a low centre of gravity and a large base.

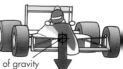

Centre of gravity

An object, like this motorcycle, will become unstable if tilted to a position where a vertical line passing through its centre of gravity falls outside the area of its base.

Centre of gravity

# Pressure

Pressure is affected by the magnitude of a force and the area over which the force acts. It is calculated with the equation:

Pressure (P) = $\dfrac{\text{force (F)}}{\text{area (A)}}$

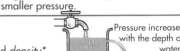

Pressure is measured in **newtons per metre² (N/m²)** with **Pascals (Pa)**.

A woman with high-heeled shoes exerts a greater pressure on the ground than if she wears flat-soled boots. Her weight

The boots exert a smaller pressure.

The high-heeled shoes exert a larger pressure.

acting on a small area produces a large pressure. Her weight acting over the larger area of the boot produces a smaller pressure.

## Pressure in liquids

Pressure in a liquid depends on its depth and *density\**. For example, as a swimmer dives to the bottom of a pool the pressure acting on him or her increases. The pressure is produced by the weight of the water above the swimmer. The more water there is, the greater the pressure it exerts. If the pure water is replaced by a denser liquid, such as sea water, the pressure exerted on the swimmer is greater.

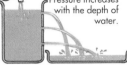

Pressure increases with the depth of water.

Pressure in liquid = depth of the liquid (h) x the density of the liquid (d) x *acceleration due to gravity (g)\**

## Hydraulic machines

*A hydraulic press*

Small force

Small piston

Large piston

Large force

Liquid

Hydraulic machines use liquids to function. Pressure acts equally in all directions throughout liquids and changes in pressure are transmitted instantly. In a hydraulic press, a small force applied to a small piston is magnified as it is transferred to a second piston with a larger surface area.

## Atmospheric pressure

Atmospheric pressure is the pressure exerted by the weight of air particles. It varies with height above the ground. A long column of air exerts a greater pressure than a short one. Atmospheric pressure is smaller on a mountain top because the air column above is shorter and the air itself is less dense. The mercury barometer and aneroid barometer measure atmospheric pressure.

## A mercury barometer

The column of mercury in a **mercury barometer** is pushed up the glass tube by air pressure. The height of the mercury column is directly affected by the magnitude of atmospheric pressure.

Atmospheric pressure can be expressed as the height of the mercury column (h).

Vacuum

Mercury

Glass tube

h

Atmospheric pressure

## An aneroid barometer

An **aneroid barometer** measures the effect of pressure on a metal box which has had some of the air removed from inside it.

If air pressure increases, the case is slightly squashed, moving the spring.

The levers translate the movement of the spring to move a pointer against a scale.

Partial vacuum

Thin metal case

Spring

Scale

Pointer

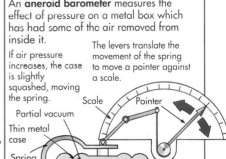

# Linear motion

Any change in an object's position is called **motion**. When a force acts on an object which is able to move, the object will begin to move in the direction in which the force is acting. If the object moves in a straight line, its motion is said to be linear.

## Speed

The **speed** of an object is defined as the distance it travels in one second. For example, the speed of a train might be 5 metres per second. If an object's speed does not change from the beginning of its journey to the end, it is moving at **constant** or **uniform speed**. If its speed constantly changes, the object's average speed can be calculated with the following equation:

Average speed = $\dfrac{\text{distance travelled}}{\text{time taken}}$

Speed is measured in **metres per second (m/s)**. It is a *scalar** quantity.

## A ticker-timer

Motion can be studied using a ticker-timer. A moving object pulls a paper tape through the timer which prints a dot on the tape every $^1/_{50}$th of a second.

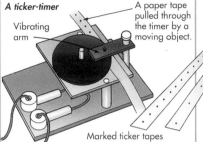

**A ticker-timer**

Vibrating arm

A paper tape pulled through the timer by a moving object.

Marked ticker tapes

The distance between the dots on a tape depends on how fast the object travels. A slow-moving object produces dots printed close together. A faster moving object produces more widely spaced dots.

## Distance/time graphs

The ticker-timer tapes produced by a moving trolley can be used to construct distance/time graphs. One dot on the tape is chosen as a starting point and the distance between this dot and successive dots is measured. This gives the distance travelled by the trolley in $^1/_{50}$th, $^2/_{50}$ths and $^3/_{50}$ths of a second and so on. When a distance/time graph is drawn, the trolley's speed at any moment is equal to the *gradient** at that point.

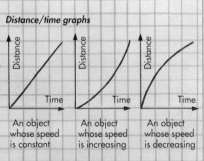

*Distance/time graphs*

An object whose speed is constant

An object whose speed is increasing

An object whose speed is decreasing

## Velocity

An object's **velocity** is a measure of how fast it travels in a given direction. Velocity is a *vector** quantity. For example, the velocity of a car might be 10 m/s north. An object whose velocity does not change is said to have a **constant velocity**. If an object's velocity is constantly changing, its **average velocity** can be calculated with the equation:

Average velocity
= $\dfrac{\text{distance travelled in a given direction}}{\text{time taken}}$

Velocity is measured in **metres per second (m/s)** in a given direction.

## Acceleration

An object is accelerating when its velocity increases. If its velocity decreases, it is decelerating. An object whose velocity is changing by the same amount in equal periods of time is said to be moving with **uniform acceleration**. Acceleration is a vector quantity and includes an indication of direction. The average acceleration of an object is calculated with the following equation:

Acceleration = $\dfrac{\text{change in velocity}}{\text{time taken for change}}$

Acceleration is measured in **metres per second per second (m/s²)**.

## Velocity/time graphs

A velocity/time graph can be constructed using ticker-tapes as shown in this diagram. The tapes are cut into strips showing 5 time intervals between them. The length of each strip is a measure of the trolley's average velocity over a $^5/_{50}$ ths of a second period (0.1 s). The trolley's acceleration at any moment is equal to the gradient of the graph at that point. The distance the trolley travels is equal to the area under the speed/time *graph* it produces.

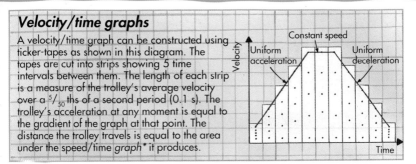

## Force, mass and acceleration

The relationship between force, mass and acceleration can be studied with the equipment shown in this diagram.

A trolley is pulled down a ramp by a fixed pulling force. This fixed force is applied by one elastic band which is stretched by a fixed amount. To calculate the trolley's acceleration, a velocity/time graph is constructed from the tape produced. The force exerted on the trolley is then doubled by using two elastic bands and the trolley's acceleration is calculated again.

The results of the experiment show that the trolley's acceleration doubles when the force doubles. This means that, if the trolley's mass remains constant, that acceleration is *directly proportional* to force.

The experiment is repeated with the force applied to the trolley kept constant, but the trolley's mass is increased by stacking another trolley on top of the first. Acceleration is calculated.

This experiment shows that, when the trolley's mass is doubled, its acceleration is halved. This means that, if the force remains constant, acceleration is *inversely proportional* to mass.

The results produced by the experiments prove the following equation:

**Force (F) = mass (m) x acceleration (a)**
(in newtons)  (in kg)  (in m/s$^2$)

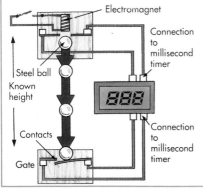

Ticker-timer

A slightly inclined ramp compensates for friction.

The trolley is pulled with an elastic band.

## The acceleration of a free-falling object

Electromagnet

Connection to millisecond timer

Steel ball

Known height

Contacts

Gate

Connection to millisecond timer

An object falling toward the ground accelerates as it falls, because of the pull of *gravity*. The value of **acceleration due to gravity (g)** can be determined using the equipment shown in the diagram. A steel ball is held by an electromagnet. A switch turns off the magnet and turns on the millisecond timer simultaneously. The ball falls a known distance, hitting a gate which turns off the timer.

The results show that the value of g at the Earth's surface is 9.8 m/s$^2$. This means that for each second an object is falling, its velocity increases by 9.8 m/s.

*Graph calculations, 55; Directly proportional, Inversely proportional, 61; Gravity, 6.

11

# Dynamics

**Dynamics** is the study of the effect of a force on the motion of an object. Newton described this relationship in three laws.

## Newton's first law

**When the forces acting on an object are equal and opposite, they cancel each other out. If the object on which they act is at rest, it will stay at rest; if it is moving, it will move at *constant velocity\*.***

For example, if a parachutist jumps from a plane, there is a period before his parachute opens, when the drag force between his body and the air balances his

A spacecraft out of reach of the Earth's gravitational pull, no forces are acting on it.

weight, and his velocity remains constant. This law also explains why a spacecraft deep in space moves at a constant velocity until a force acts on it. This force could come from having its engines fired, or from entering the *gravitational field\** of a planet.

## Newton's second law

**If an unbalanced force acts on an object, it accelerates in the direction in which the force acts. The object's acceleration is directly proportional to the force, if its mass remains constant.**

For example, the constant force produced by the rocket engines of a spacecraft makes it *accelerate\**. The acceleration doubles if the force of the

engines doubles. Newton's second law is also demonstrated by the ticker-timer and trolley experiment (page 11) which proved the equation:

Force = mass x acceleration.

This is an important statement of Newton's second law. It produces the definition of a newton as the force which gives a mass of 1 kg an acceleration of 1 $m/s^2$.

## Newton's third law

The force of the football on the ground

The upward force of the ground on the football

**For every force there is an equal and opposite force called a reaction force.**

Newton's third law shows that forces always occur in pairs. When one object (A) exerts a force on another object (B), object B exerts an equal but opposite force on A. For example, if a person on roller skates pushes someone else on roller skates, both skaters will move away from each other in opposite directions. The equal and opposite forces do not cancel each other out, because each force is acting on a different object.

## Momentum

The **momentum** of an object is its mass multiplied by its velocity. Momentum is a *vector\** quantity. A car of mass 1,500 kg travelling at a velocity of 10 m/s has a momentum of 15,000 kg m/s.

When two objects collide they apply equal and opposite forces to each other. One object may gain an amount of momentum equal to the amount the other object loses, but their total momentum remains the same before and after the collision. This is a statement of the **principle of conservation of momentum.**

Before collision the cars' total momentum = $m_1u_1 + m_2u_2$

The moving car has a velocity $u_1$.

The stationary car has a velocity $u_2$.

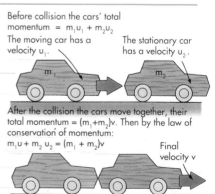

After the collision the cars move together, their total momentum = $(m_1+m_2)v$. Then by the law of conservation of momentum:
$m_1u + m_2 u_2 = (m_1 + m_2)v$

Final velocity v

*Constant velocity, Acceleration, 10; Gravitational field, 6; Vectors, 7.

# Energy

Everything needs **energy** to function. Creatures need the energy stored in food to carry out their vital functions. Machines need the energy stored in chemical fuels to perform tasks. All forms of energy are measured in **joules (J)**.

## Different forms of energy

Energy exists in many forms. *Heat\*, sound\*, nuclear energy\*, electromagnetic radiation\** and *electrical energy\** are all forms of energy and each is looked at in detail later in this book.

**Potential energy** is the energy an object has because of its position. It is energy which has been stored.

**Gravitational potential energy** is an example of potential energy. It is the energy an object has because of its position above the Earth. The further above the Earth it is, the more gravitational potential energy it stores up. For example, a diver on a high board has more gravitational potential energy than she has when standing on the ground. When she dives and returns to ground level, she loses her gravitational potential energy.

**Elastic energy** is the potential energy some materials have when they are squashed or stretched. They have the potential energy to spring back to their normal shape. For example, a spring has elastic energy when it is squashed.

**Chemical energy** is stored energy which is released during some chemical reactions. Coal and wood contain chemical energy and produce heat when burnt. Cells contain chemical energy which is used to produce electrical energy.

**Kinetic energy** is the energy possessed by any object because it is moving. For example, a swing has kinetic energy when it is moving.

As the swing moves, energy is continually converted from potential energy, at the top of its swinging motion, to kinetic energy at the bottom of its swinging motion.

## Energy conversion

When energy changes from one form to another it is called **energy conversion**. For example, the diver's potential energy is converted into kinetic energy as she dives. If a number of energy changes take place, an energy chain is produced.

The source of most of the energy on Earth is the Sun. In most energy chains the last form of the energy is heat. The diagram below shows the chain of energy conversions which take place in a coal-fired power station.

Fossil fuels store chemical energy.

Furnace - Fuel is burnt to produce heat energy.

Steam driven turbines produce kinetic energy.

Dynamo - Kinetic energy is used to produce electrical energy.

Appliances - Electricity produces heat, light and sound.

## The law of conservation of energy

The law of conservation of energy states that **energy cannot be created or destroyed, only converted from one form to another.** At any stage in a chain of energy conversion the number of joules of energy present is the same, because the total amount of energy in existence cannot alter.

*Heat, 26; Sound, 18; Nuclear energy, 44; Electromagnetic radiation, 45; Electrical energy, 32.

# Work, energy and machines

**Work** is done when a force is applied to an object and the object moves in the direction the force is acting. For example, work is done when a crate is lifted or a car is pushed. However, if a crate is too heavy to be lifted, or if the person pushing the car is unable to get the car moving, no work is done.

To calculate the amount of work done when a force moves an object, the magnitude of the force is multiplied by the distance the object is moved. This is written as follows:

**Work (W) = force (F) x distance object moves in direction of force (d)**

Work is measured in **joules (J)**. 1 J of work is done when a force of 1 N moves an object a distance of 1 m.

## Work and energy

Energy is needed for work to be done. For example, if an object A exerts a force on another object B, and B moves, then work has been done by A on B and energy has been transferred from A to B. The amount of energy transferred is equal to the amount of work done.

## Lifting

Work is done when an object is lifted off the ground against the force of gravity. The object which is lifted gains *potential energy*\* as the work is done. The amount of potential energy the object gains is calculated with the equation:

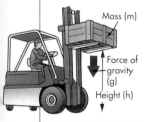

Mass (m)

Force of gravity (g)

Height (h)

**Potential energy (P.E.) = weight (mg) x height raised (h)**
This can also be written as follows:
**P.E. = mgh**

## Pushing and pulling

Work is done when an object is pushed or pulled and it moves. For example, when the man below pushes the car, the car starts to move, gaining *kinetic energy*\*. The amount of kinetic energy it gains is calculated with the following equation:

**Kinetic energy (K.E.)
= ½ mass (m) x velocity² (v²)**
This can also be written as follows:
**K.E. = ½ mv²**

The man must do work to overcome the force of friction between the car's tyres and the ground.

## Non-renewable sources of energy

*Electrical energy*\* is essential to many aspects of human activity. A variety of fuel sources are used to generate electrical energy. Fossil fuels, such as coal, oil and natural gas, are called **non-renewable energy sources**. They were laid down under the Earth's surface millions of years ago.

At present these resources are in plentiful supply, but once used up, they cannot be replaced. Energy-saving measures, ranging from increasing the efficiency of machines to insulating homes to reduce heat loss, will help preserve non-renewable resources.

## Renewable sources of energy

Some sources of energy, such as the Sun, are virtually inexhaustible. These are called **renewable energy sources**. Solar power can be converted into electrical energy in solar furnaces or solar powered homes. Other renewable energy sources include geothermal power (heat energy from the centre of the Earth), wind and wave power. Renewable energy soruces will become more and more important in the future.

Windmills gain kinetic energy from the wind.

\*Potential energy, Kinetic energy, Electrical energy, 13.

## Machines

The force applied to a machine is called the **effort**. The force moved by an effort is called the **load**. Machines are used in many different situations to make work easier. They achieve this by magnifying the effect of an effort. In this way, a small effort can be used to overcome a much greater load.

## A pulley

A **pulley** is a machine made up of one or more wheels and a rope, belt or chain. A small effort applied to a pulley system can lift a heavy load. However, in order to do this, the effort has to move a

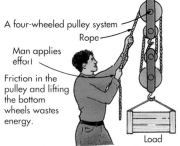

A four-wheeled pulley system
Rope
Man applies effort
Friction in the pulley and lifting the bottom wheels wastes energy.
Load

greater distance than the load. In the pulley system shown above, the effort must move far enough to shorten all four strings of the lower part of the pulley before it lifts the load.

## Power

The **power** of a person or a machine is a measure of how quickly they do work or the rate at which they change one form of energy into another. Power is calculated with the following equation:

$$Power (P) = \frac{work\ done\ (W)}{time\ taken\ (t)}$$

Power is measured in **watts (W)**. 1 W is equal to 1 joule of work done in 1 second. Large quantities of power are measured in kilowatts (1,000 watts) and megawatts (1,000,000 watts).

The power output of a system like the

human body can be calculated with the following equation:

$$Power\ output = \frac{force\ x\ distance\ moved}{time\ taken}$$

For example, if a boy weighing 600 N runs up a flight of stairs (vertical height of 3 m) in 6 seconds, his power output is calculated as follows:

Power output
$$= \frac{600 \times 3}{6}$$
$$= 300\ watts$$

Height

## Efficiency of a machine

**Efficiency** is a measure of how good a machine is at doing its job. Machines are never perfectly efficient. When they convert one form of energy to another form, some of the energy supplied by the effort is not changed into the required form. This means for all machines, the work output is less than the work input. For example, the man lifting a crate (shown at the top of this page) not only lifts the weight of the crate, he also lifts the weight of the lower wheels and the rope of the pulley. In addition he does work to overcome the frictional forces which exist between the moving parts of the pulley system. This wasted energy reduces the efficiency of the pulley.

Efficiency is usually expressed as a percentage. A 'perfect machine' which

did not waste any energy would be 100% efficient. Efficiency is calculated with any of the following equations:

$$Efficiency = \frac{work\ output}{work\ input} \times 100$$
or
$$= \frac{energy\ output}{energy\ input} \times 100$$
or
$$= \frac{power\ output}{power\ input} \times 100$$

For example, if the man using the pulley system exerts a 200 N effort through a distance of 2 m, to lift a 600 N load a height of 0.5 m, his work input is 400 J (200 x 2). The machine's work output is 300 J (600 x 0.5).

The pulley system's efficiency
$$= \frac{300}{400} \times 100$$
$$= 75\%$$

*Friction, 6.

# Waves

When an object disturbs the *medium\** around it, the disturbance travels away from the source in the form of **waves.** Waves which transport energy away from a source are called **progressive waves**. A wave does not permanently disturb the medium through which it travels. For example, as a wave passes along the surface of water, the water particles vibrate up and down. They do not travel with the wave; they eventually return to their original positions. Waves are either **longitudinal** or **transverse**, depending on the vibrations which cause them.

## Transverse waves

In a transverse wave the vibrations which form the wave move at right angles to the direction in which the wave is travelling. Water waves have a transverse motion.

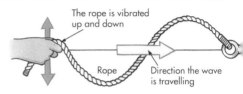

The rope is vibrated up and down

Rope

Direction the wave is travelling

## Longitudinal waves

A longitudinal wave is one in which the particles vibrate in the same direction as the wave is travelling. As a vibrating object moves forwards, it squashes the particles of a medium together to form **compressions**. When the object moves backwards, the particles of the medium become widely spaced, forming **rarefactions**. The compressions and rarefactions produced both travel away from the object. *Sound waves\** have a longitudinal wave motion.

Compression          Rarefaction          Direction the wave is travelling

The coil is vibrated backwards and forwards.

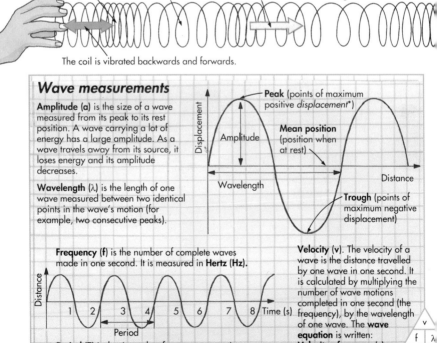

## Wave measurements

**Amplitude (a)** is the size of a wave measured from its peak to its rest position. A wave carrying a lot of energy has a large amplitude. As a wave travels away from its source, it loses energy and its amplitude decreases.

**Wavelength (λ)** is the length of one wave measured between two identical points in the wave's motion (for example, two consecutive peaks).

Displacement

**Peak** (points of maximum positive *displacement\**)

Amplitude

**Mean position** (position when at rest)

Wavelength

Distance

**Trough** (points of maximum negative displacement)

**Frequency (f)** is the number of complete waves made in one second. It is measured in **Hertz (Hz).**

Distance

1  2  3  4  5  6  7  8  Time (s)

Period

**Period (T)** is the time taken for one wave motion to be completed. It is measured in seconds.

**Velocity (v).** The velocity of a wave is the distance travelled by one wave in one second. It is calculated by multiplying the number of wave motions completed in one second (the frequency), by the wavelength of one wave. The **wave equation** is written:

Velocity of a wave (v) = frequency (f) x wavelength (λ)

$$\frac{v}{f \quad λ}$$

*Medium, 61; Sound waves, 18; Displacement, 61.

## The behaviour of waves

The behaviour of waves is studied using a **ripple tank**. This is a shallow tank of water, with a lamp above which casts shadows on to a piece of paper below the tank. A bar in the tank produces the straight-fronted waves shown below.

## Reflection

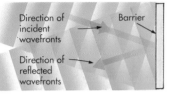

A wave is **reflected** when it bounces off a barrier. Before reflection the waves are called incident waves and, after reflection, reflected waves. The angle at which incident waves hit a barrier is equal to the angle at which they are reflected. All waves experience reflection, including light and sound waves.

## Refraction

**Refraction** is the change in the direction of a wave as it passes from one medium to another. Refraction is caused by the wave changing speed as it passes into the new medium. If, for example, water waves in a ripple tank pass from deep water into shallow water they change speed and direction as shown in the diagram. Light waves are also refracted when they pass between different media.

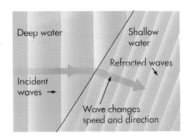

## Diffraction

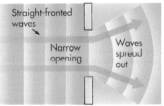

**Diffraction** occurs when waves bend around a barrier or spread out after passing through a gap. Waves are diffracted most when the gap through which they pass is about the same size as their wavelength. For example, sound waves have a long wavelength and are diffracted by large gaps. Light waves have a short wavelength, and are diffracted by a very tiny gap.

## Wave interference

**Wave interference** occurs when two waves combine with each other. When the waves have the same frequency and direction, and peak and trough at the same time, they are said to be 'in phase'. The combined amplitude of two in phase waves is larger than for a single wave. This is called **constructive interference**.

**Destructive interference** occurs when 'out of phase' waves meet. They peak and trough at different times. The amplitude of their resultant wave is smaller than that of the waves before they meet. Constructive interference of light waves causes patches of bright light, and destructive interference produces patches of darkness.

*Constructive interference*
Waves in phase

Resultant wave has greater amplitude

*Destructive interference*
Waves out of phase

Waves cancel each other out

# Sound

**Sound** is produced by vibrating objects such as musical instruments and the vocal cords which produce a human voice. Sound waves are *longitudinal waves** which carry vibrations from a sound source. A vibrating object disturbs the medium which surrounds it by moving backwards and forwards producing compressions and rarefactions in the particles of the medium.

Sound waves need the particles of a medium to travel through. For example,

The tuning fork's prongs vibrate.

Compression    Rarefaction    Human ear

a bell ringing in a jar from which the air has been removed cannot be heard. It is silent on the Moon because there is no atmosphere and, therefore, no medium.

## The speed of sound

Sound waves travel at different speeds through different media. They travel fastest through solids, and faster through liquids than gases. When a sound wave hits an obstruction it may be reflected. This is called an **echo**. The speed of sound in air can be measured by a simple method using echoes.

To calculate the speed of sound in air, stand 100 m away from a wall which has no other walls or trees nearby. Clap your hands and listen for the echo. Practice clapping rhythmically until the echo cannot be heard because it coincides exactly with the next clap. Time how long it takes to clap 20 times.

*Experiment to calculate the speed of sound*

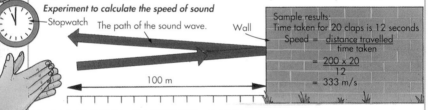

Stopwatch    The path of the sound wave.    Wall

100 m

Sample results:
Time taken for 20 claps is 12 seconds

$$Speed = \frac{distance\ travelled}{time\ taken}$$

$$= \frac{200 \times 20}{12}$$

$$= 333\ m/s$$

## The shape of sound

The shapes of different sound waves can be compared by feeding them into a microphone and displaying them on the screen of a *cathode ray oscilloscope**.

## Loudness and amplitude

Large amplitude    Small amplitude

Loud note    Soft note

A sound can be loud or soft depending on the *amplitude** of its wave. A sound with a large amplitude is carrying a lot of energy and will be loud. A sound with a small amplitude will be soft.

## Pitch and frequency

High frequency    Low frequency

High pitch    Low pitch

If a musical note has a sound wave with a high *frequency**, it will have a high pitch. Many musical instruments can produce similar pitches, but they sound very different from one another. This is because each instrument produces other frequencies called **overtones** which change the shape of a sound wave. Overtones vary according to the size, shape and construction of an instrument.

*Longitudinal waves, 16; Cathode ray oscilloscope, 48; Amplitude, Frequency, 16.

# Light

**Light** is a form of energy emitted by luminous objects such as the Sun or candles. An object which emits light is called a **source**. A few living creatures, such as fireflies, glow worms and some deep-water fish, produce their own light.

Most objects are non-luminous and can only be seen because light from another source bounces off them into the eye. For example, you can see this page because daylight or lamplight is bouncing off it into your eyes. Light energy is carried from a source by waves. Light waves are part of the *electromagnetic spectrum**. They travel in straight lines away from their source. This is called **rectilinear propagation**. In diagrams light is represented by straight lines called rays. An arrow on a ray indicates the direction in which the light is travelling.

## Shadows

If light rays from a small source hit an object in their path, a sharp edged shadow or **umbra** is formed. The umbra appears behind the object in the area that no light has reached.

If the source of light is large, a shadow with blurred edges, called a **penumbra**, is formed around the umbra. A penumbra is an area of less sharp shadow, which a small amount of light has reached.

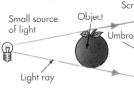

Small source of light · Object · Screen · Umbra · Light ray

Large light source · Object · Penumbra · Umbra · light ray

## Eclipses

When the Moon moves to a position directly between the Sun and the Earth, it casts a circular shadow on the Earth's surface. This is called a **solar eclipse**. This diagram is not drawn to scale.

Viewed from the umbra, no light from the Sun can be seen. This is called a **total eclipse**.

Sun · Moon · Earth · Umbra · Penumbra · Light ray

Viewed from the penumbra, some light from the Sun is seen. This is called a **partial eclipse**.

## A pinhole camera

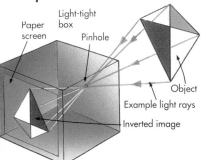

Paper screen · Light-tight box · Pinhole · Object · Example light rays · Inverted image

A pinhole camera is the simplest form of camera. It can be made from an ordinary box with a tracing paper screen. Light rays from an object enter the box, crossing over as they pass through a pinhole in the side of the box. This produces an upside down *image** on a screen. If the object is moved nearer to the camera, the image becomes larger. If the screen is replaced with photographic paper, a permanent picture of the object will be formed.

*Electromagnetic spectrum, 45; Image, 20.

# The reflection of light

Reflection of light occurs when a light ray hits a surface and bounces off, changing direction. Mirrors are usually used to demonstrate the reflection of light because their shiny surfaces reflect more light than dull, rough surfaces.

Reflected light always obeys two laws, called the **laws of reflection**. These state:

**1. The incident ray, the reflected ray and the normal are all in the same plane.**

**2. The angle of incidence is equal to the angle of reflection.**

The diagram shows light being reflected and identifies the terms used above.

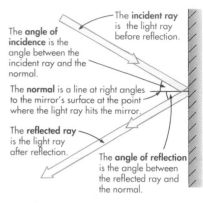

The **incident ray** is the light ray before reflection.

The **angle of incidence** is the angle between the incident ray and the normal.

The **normal** is a line at right angles to the mirror's surface at the point where the light ray hits the mirror.

The **reflected ray** is the light ray after reflection.

The **angle of reflection** is the angle between the reflected ray and the normal.

## Real and virtual images

There are two types of image; real and virtual. A **virtual** image is formed when, for example, light rays from an object placed in front of a mirror are reflected into the human eye. The eye sees an image of the object behind the surface of the mirror. The image is called a virtual image, because the light rays only appear to come from it.

A **real** image is formed when rays from an object actually pass through the image, as in the *pinhole camera**. A real image produces a photographic image if film is placed where the image forms. The image projected onto the screen at the cinema is a real image.

## Reflection in a plane mirror

The image formed by reflection in a plane mirror is always virtual and erect (the same way up as the object). It is the same distance behind the mirror as the object is in front. The image is laterally inverted, which means that the left side is interchanged with the right.

It is possible to construct a ray diagram to find the position of the virtual image formed by an object in front of a mirror. The steps below should be followed carefully to produce an accurate diagram.

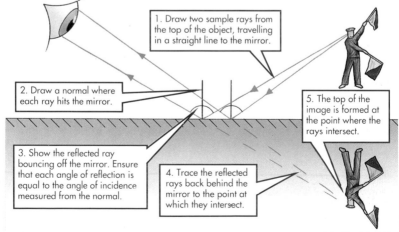

1. Draw two sample rays from the top of the object, travelling in a straight line to the mirror.

2. Draw a normal where each ray hits the mirror.

3. Show the reflected ray bouncing off the mirror. Ensure that each angle of reflection is equal to the angle of incidence measured from the normal.

4. Trace the reflected rays back behind the mirror to the point at which they intersect.

5. The top of the image is formed at the point where the rays intersect.

# The refraction of light

When a light ray passes from one *medium**
to another it changes direction. This is
called **refraction**. Refraction is caused by
the light wave changing speed as it passes
into the new medium.

For example, a ray passing from one
medium into an optically more dense
medium (such as from air into glass), slows
down and bends toward the normal. A ray
passing into an optically less dense medium
speeds up, bending away from the normal.

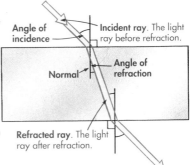

**Angle of incidence**

**Incident ray**. The light ray before refraction.

**Angle of refraction**

**Normal**

**Refracted ray**. The light ray after refraction.

## The critical angle

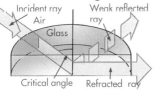

Incident ray
Air
Glass
Weak reflected ray
Critical angle
Refracted ray

If a light ray emerging from glass into air skims
along the surface of the glass, its angle of
incidence is called the **critical angle**. The ray is
refracted at 90° to the normal. A small amount of
light is reflected at the boundary and passes back
into the glass. A light ray passing into any optically
less dense medium will behave in this way.

## Total internal reflection

If a light ray which hits the boundary between
glass and air has an angle of incidence greater
than the critical angle it is not refracted. All the
light is reflected back inside the denser medium.
This is called **total internal reflection**.

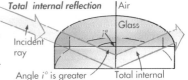

*Total internal reflection* | Air
Glass
Incident ray
Angle $i°$ is greater than the critical angle.
Total internal reflected ray

### Right angled prisms

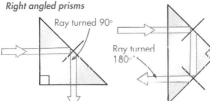

Ray turned 90°
Ray turned 180°

**Right angled prisms** use total internal
reflection to alter the path of light, turning it
through 90° or 180°. These prisms are used in
periscopes, binoculars and cameras.

**Optical fibres** use total internal
reflection to transmit light along a
glass or plastic tube. They are used in
medicine and telecommunications.

*An optical fibre*

Glass fibres
Path of light ray

## Colour and the spectrum

White light is made up of different colours
of light. When a ray of white light is
shone through a glass prism it splits into a
rainbow of colours called the **spectrum**.
The splitting of light in this way is called
**dispersion**. Dispersion is caused by the
different colours of light travelling at
slightly different speeds in glass or water.
Each of the colours is refracted by slightly
different amounts.

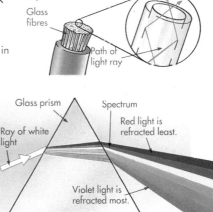

Glass prism
Spectrum
Red light is refracted least.
Ray of white light
Violet light is refracted most.

*Medium, 61.

# Lenses and optical instruments

A **lens** is a piece of glass with curved surfaces. When light is refracted by a lens an image is formed. There are two main types of lens: **converging** lenses which have outward curving surfaces, and **diverging** lenses which have inward curving surfaces. Lenses are used in a variety of optical instruments.

## A converging lens

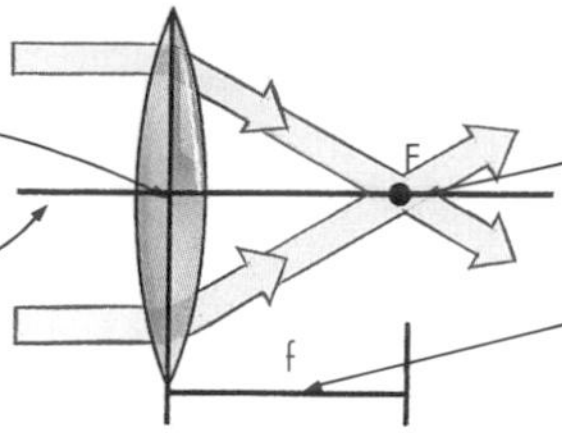

The **optical centre** is the centre of the lens. Rays travelling through the optical centre pass straight through the lens.

The **principal axis** is an imaginary line through the optical centre of the lens at right angles to the lens.

The **principal focus** (F) is the point at which all rays travelling parallel to the principal axis intersect after refraction.

The **focal length** (f) is the distance from the optical centre to the principal focus.

## Measuring the focal length of a converging lens

A converging lens is held between a screen and a distant light source, such as a window. The distance between lens and screen is adjusted until a clear image of the window forms on the screen. Because the window is distant, the light rays from a point on it are almost parallel to each other when they reach the lens. This means that the image is formed roughly at the principal focus of the lens. The focal length is the distance between the lens's optical centre and the image.

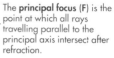

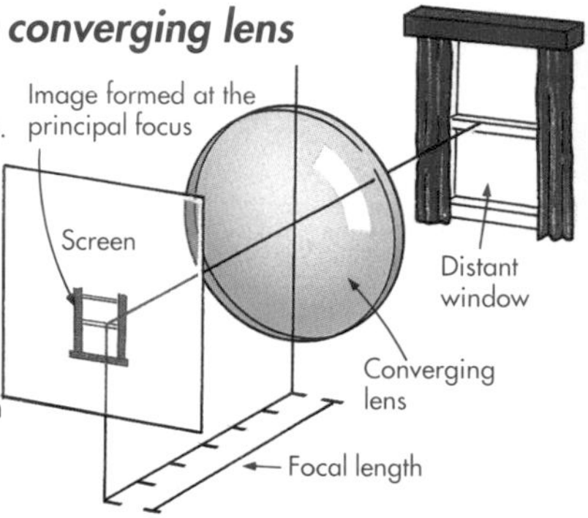

Image formed at the principal focus

Screen

Distant window

Converging lens

Focal length

## Image formation with a lens

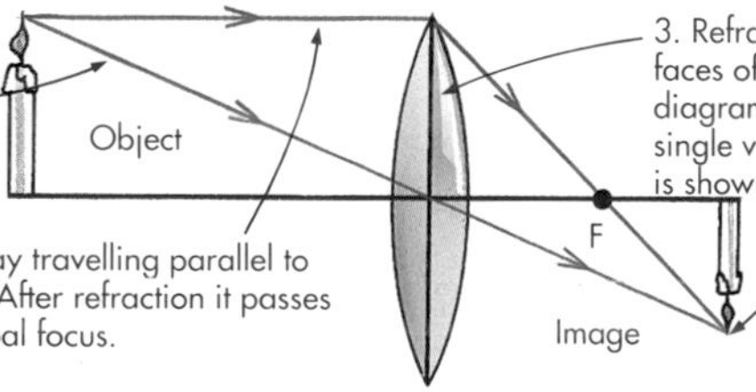

1. Draw one ray straight through the optical centre. It is not refracted.

Object

2. Draw another ray travelling parallel to the principal axis. After refraction it passes through the principal focus.

F

Image

3. Refraction takes place at both faces of the lens, but on a ray diagram the lens is replaced by a single vertical line and refraction is shown at this line only.

4. The top of the image is formed where the two rays intersect.

## Optical instruments

Optical instruments contain one or more lenses to produce a specific type of image. For example, a camera uses a converging lens to form a real, diminished (smaller than the object), inverted image on photographic film.

A slide projector uses converging lenses to form a real, magnified, inverted image of a photographic slide on a screen. A magnifying glass is a converging lens which produces a magnified, erect, virtual image as shown in the ray diagram below.

A page of text viewed through a magnifying glass.

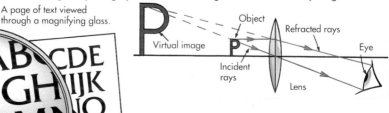

Object

Virtual image

Refracted rays

Eye

Incident rays

Lens

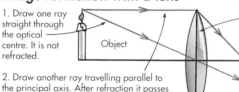

# The eye and the ear

## The human eye

The eye is a highly developed optical instrument. Light rays are refracted by the **cornea** and the **lens** to form an image on the **retina**. The retina, made of light sensitive cells, changes light into electric signals which are sent to the brain by the **optic nerve**. The *focal length** of the lens depends on its shape. The lens's shape is controlled by a ring of muscle called the **ciliary muscle**. When the eye looks at distant objects, the muscle relaxes. The ring becomes larger, tightening the **fibres of the suspensory ligament**. This flattens the lens, giving it a long focal length. When viewing close objects, the muscle contracts, the fibres relax and the lens becomes fatter, with a short focal length.

A **short-sighted** person has difficulty focusing on distant objects because the light rays are focused in front of the retina. In glasses and contact lenses, a

The coloured **iris** contains a hole called the **pupil**. In bright light, the iris expands to reduce the pupil's size and let in less light. In dim light it contracts to increase the pupil's size and let in more light.

The lens is the fine focusing component of the eye.

The transparent cornea is one of the focusing components of the eye.

Fibres of the suspensory ligament  Ciliary muscle  Retina  Optic nerve

diverging lens is used to correct this. A **long-sighted** person has difficulty focusing on close objects because the light rays are focused behind the retina. A converging lens is used to correct this.

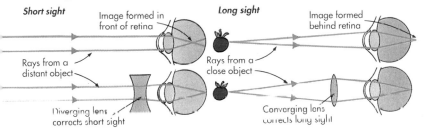

**Short sight**
Image formed in front of retina
Rays from a distant object
Diverging lens corrects short sight

**Long sight**
Image formed behind retina
Rays from a close object
Converging lens corrects long sight

## The human ear

Sound waves travel down the **ear canal** to the **ear drum**. The ear drum vibrates at the same *frequency** as the sound waves. The vibrations are then transferred by a chain of three bones in the **middle ear**, called the **ossicles**, to the **oval window**. The ossicles and the oval window increase

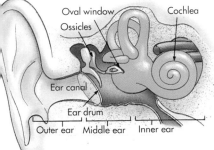

Oval window  Cochlea
Ossicles
Ear canal
Ear drum
Outer ear  Middle ear  Inner ear

the amplitude of the vibrations. In the **inner ear** the vibrations pass along the **cochlea** where sound waves of different frequencies stimulate different nerves. The nerves change sound waves into electrical signals, which are sent to the brain.

Humans can hear frequencies ranging from 20 Hz to 20,000 Hz. Sounds above 20,000 Hz are called **ultrasound** and can be heard by some animals, such as bats.

Old age leads to an inability to hear high frequency sounds. Listening to loud sounds can damage the sensory cells in the cochlea and result in an inability to hear certain frequencies.

Poor hearing can be improved with a hearing aid, which increases the *amplitude** of sound waves.

*Focal length, 22; Frequency, Amplitude, 16.    23

# The Earth in space

Developments in science and technology have led to space travel, advanced communication systems and the chance to study the Earth from space.

Astronomers think the **Universe** began about 15,000 million years ago with a huge explosion, called the **Big Bang**. Before the Big Bang all the matter in the Universe is thought to have been concentrated into a very small volume.

The explosion sent matter flying out in all directions. This matter later formed **stars** and **planets**. The **galaxies**, which are huge collections of stars, are still moving away from each other today as a result of the explosion. No one knows whether the Universe will continue to expand forever, or whether *gravitational forces of attraction** will start to pull the galaxies back towards each other.

## The Milky Way

The Milky Way is the galaxy in which the Earth lies. It is just one of millions of galaxies that make up the Universe. On a clear night the other stars of the Milky Way can be seen as a faint band of light in the sky.

The **Sun** is a star like the millions of other stars in the Milky Way.

The Milky Way is spiral shaped and formed from an estimated 100,000 million stars.

## The Solar System

The Sun lies at the centre of our Solar System which is made up of nine known major planets, including the Earth.

A **satellite** is an object in space, such as a moon, which orbits another larger object like a planet. Many planets have their own natural satellites.

Also orbiting the Sun are large numbers of lumps of rock, called **asteroids**, and balls of frozen gas and rock called **comets**. When comets get near the Sun, the ice *vaporizes**, leaving a trail of gas and dust.

## The Earth's motion

The Earth takes 365.26 days to travel once around the Sun. The shape of its orbit is 'elliptical', which is like a slightly squashed circle. As the Earth orbits the Sun, it spins on its **axis** once every twenty-four hours. The axis is an imaginary line which runs through the Earth from the North Pole to the South Pole. As it orbits the Sun, the Earth is not completely upright. Its axis is tilted at an angle of approximately 23° to the plane of its orbit.

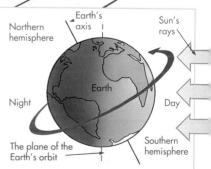

Earth's axis
Northern hemisphere
Sun's rays
Night
Earth
Day
The plane of the Earth's orbit
Southern hemisphere

*Gravitational forces, 6; Vaporizes, 61.

## Seasonal changes

The inclination of the Earth's axis causes seasonal changes and a variation in the number of daylight hours in a day. Summer is the period during which the land is inclined towards the Sun and the Sun's rays hit the ground almost perpendicularly. When it is summer in the northern hemisphere, it is winter in the southern hemisphere and vice versa. In winter, the Sun's rays slant across the Earth's surface. Their heat is spread over a larger area, weakening their intensity.

The length of a day is governed by the Sun's position in the sky. Due to the inclination of the land during summer, the Sun gets higher in the sky and is visible longer. In winter it is lower in the sky, rising above the horizon later in the day and disappearing earlier.

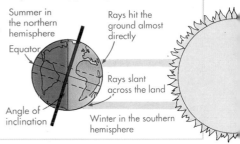

Summer in the northern hemisphere

Equator

Angle of inclination

Rays hit the ground almost directly

Rays slant across the land

Winter in the southern hemisphere

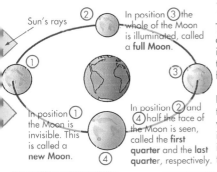

Sun's rays

In position ② the whole of the Moon is illuminated, called a **full Moon**.

In position ① the Moon is invisible. This is called a **new Moon**.

In position ② and ④ half the face of the Moon is seen, called the **first quarter** and the **last quarter**, respectively.

## The Moon's motion

The Earth has one moon which orbits it once every 27.3 days. The Moon spins on its axis once during this orbit. This means that the same half of the Moon is always facing the Earth.

The Moon does not produce its own light. It is visible because it *reflects** light from the Sun. The part of the Moon which is visible from Earth depends on its position in relation to the Sun. The different illuminated sections of the Moon shown in the diagram are called its **phases**.

## The effects of gravity

There is a strong force of gravitational attraction which exists between two objects the size of planets and stars. Gravity keeps the planets in orbit around the Sun, and the Moon in orbit around the Earth.

The Moon is constantly moving forward in a straight line. It would move further away into space if the Earth did not exert a gravitational force which pulls it back in the direction of the Earth's centre. The effect of this gravitational pull acting at right angles to the Moon's motion produces the circular orbit of the Moon.

Gravity also affects the seas and oceans on Earth. The gravitational force exerted by the Moon on the Earth attracts the water on the side of the Earth it faces. This causes a bulge in the water's surface

called a **high tide**. There are two high tides and two **low tides** every twenty-four hours. When the Sun is in line with the Moon, the combined gravitational force on the water is greater, producing higher tides called **spring tides**.

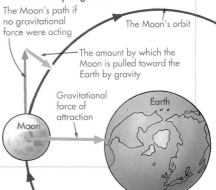

The Moon's path if no gravitational force were acting

The Moon's orbit

The amount by which the Moon is pulled toward the Earth by gravity

Gravitational force of attraction

Moon

Earth

*Reflection, 20.

Heat is a form of energy. When a substance is supplied with heat energy, its molecules gain *kinetic energy** from the heat source and move at a greater speed. The faster they move, the hotter the substance becomes. The substance is said to have gained **internal energy**.

**Temperature** is a measurement of how hot or cold a substance is. It does not mean the same thing as 'heat'. It depends on the average speed of the molecules in a substance. For example, a hot spark of magnesium has a higher temperature than a mug of boiling water, because its molecules are moving faster. However, the water has more heat energy than the spark because it has more molecules and their total energy is greater.

## Thermometers

Temperature is measured using a **thermometer**. Thermometers contain substances which change when heated. Some contain liquids which expand when heated. For example, if a 'liquid-in-glass' thermometer is placed in a hot substance, the liquid inside it will expand and rise up the tube. Alcohol and mercury are commonly used in these thermometers. Alcohol freezes at a lower temperature than mercury and is used to measure very low temperatures, for instance at the North and South Poles. Other thermometers include the resistance thermometer, which contains a wire whose *resistance** to electric current changes if its temperature changes.

## A clinical thermometer

A clinical thermometer is used to measure the small variations in the temperature of the human body.

The triangular glass acts as a magnifying glass.

A constriction in the tube prevents mercury returning to the bulb before a reading can be taken. The thermometer must be shaken to force the mercury back into the bulb.

The scale is calibrated in degrees Celsius, between 35 °C and 42 °C

A narrow tube ensures the mercury moves a visible distance even for very small changes in temperature.

## The Celsius temperature scale

The **Celsius scale** has two fixed points. The lower one (0 °C), called the ice point, is the melting point of pure ice. The upper one (100 °C), called the steam point, is the temperature of the steam above water, which is boiling at normal atmospheric pressure. One hundred divisions are made between these points, called **degrees Celsius (°C)**.

*Finding the fixed points to calibrate a Celsius scale on a thermometer*

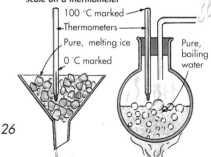

100 °C marked
Thermometers
Pure, melting ice
0 °C marked
Pure, boiling water

## The absolute temperature scale

The **absolute temperature** scale starts at a point called **absolute zero**. This is the lowest temperature theoretically achievable. It is the point at which no more heat energy can be removed from a substance. Measured in degrees Celsius, absolute zero is −273 °C. The absolute scale uses units called **kelvins (K)**. Kelvins are the same size as degrees Celsius.

## How to convert between degrees Celsius and kelvins

To convert a temperature from degrees Celsius to kelvins, add 273 to the Celsius temperature. For example, 0 °C is 273 K, 50 °C is 323 K and 100 °C is 373 K. To convert a temperature from kelvins to degrees Celsius, subtract 273 from the temperature in kelvins. For example, 200 K is −73 °C, 300 K is 27 °C.

*Kinetic energy, 13; Resistance, 34.

# Heat and expansion

Most substances increase in size when heated. This is called **expansion**. The molecules in the substance gain kinetic energy and begin to move faster. They are able to make larger vibrations and push each other further and further apart, causing the substance to enlarge.

## The expansion of solids and liquids

Solids will only expand by a very small amount. This is because their molecules are held together by strong forces of attraction. Most liquids expand more than solids because their molecules have more energy to break free of the forces which attract them to their neighbours.

## A bimetallic strip

Different solids expand at different rates. This is demonstrated in the behaviour of a **bimetallic strip**, which is used in thermostats to regulate temperature in central heating systems.

A bimetallic strip is a strip of copper and iron fixed firmly together.

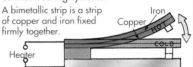

When heated, copper expands more than iron. This causes the strip to bend outwards breaking the electrical circuit and turning off the heater. When it cools the strip bends back and the heater is switched on.

## The expansion of gases

The volume of a gas is affected both by heating and by the pressure exerted on it. Therefore, when studying the expansion of gases, three variables must be considered: temperature, volume and pressure.

### Gas at constant temperature

If the volume of a gas is decreased, its pressure increases. The pressure in a gas depends on the rate at which its molecules hit the sides of the container. As volume decreases, the gas molecules are pushed closer together. Although they are moving at the same speed, they hit the container's walls more often, increasing the gas's internal pressure.

### Gas at constant volume

If a gas is heated, but not allowed to expand, its internal pressure increases. This means the gas molecules gain kinetic energy from the heat source and hit the walls of their container more violently and more often.

### Gas at constant pressure

A gas at constant pressure expands when heated because its molecules gain kinetic energy. The internal pressure of the gas remains constant because the molecules hit the walls of their container at the same rate because they have more space to move in.

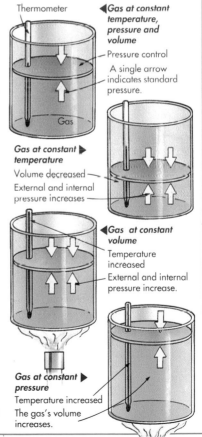

◄ Gas at constant temperature, pressure and volume

Pressure control

A single arrow indicates standard pressure.

Gas at constant ► temperature

Volume decreased

External and internal pressure increases

◄ Gas at constant volume

Temperature increased

External and internal pressure increase.

Gas at constant ► pressure

Temperature increased

The gas's volume increases.

If a temperature difference exists between two places, heat energy is transferred from the hotter to the cooler place. This heat transfer continues until the temperature is the same in both places.

Heat can travel in three ways: by **conduction**, **convection** and **radiation**. It is important to be able to recognize which of these three processes is taking place in any given situation.

## Conduction

Conduction is the transfer of heat, from *molecule** to molecule, throughout a material. The molecules inside the material which are nearest to a heat source gain *kinetic energy**. They vibrate vigorously, and their movement affects the molecules immediately next to them. They pass on some of their energy, spreading heat through the material. Conduction is chiefly associated with solids, because the closely packed molecular structure of a solid is most suited to it.

Metals are very good conductors of heat. They conduct heat rapidly, because they contain 'free' electrons*. The free

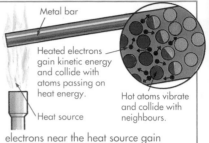

Metal bar

Heated electrons gain kinetic energy and collide with atoms passing on heat energy.

Heat source

Hot atoms vibrate and collide with neighbours.

electrons near the heat source gain energy and move rapidly throughout the metal. They collide with atoms, passing on their kinetic energy. Saucepans, radiators and central heating pipes are made of metallic materials to ensure rapid heat conduction.

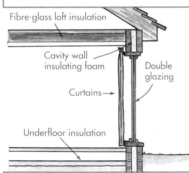

Fibre-glass loft insulation

Cavity wall insulating foam

Double glazing

Curtains

Underfloor insulation

## Insulation

Substances which conduct heat slowly, such as wood and water, are called **insulators**. Air is one of the best insulators of heat. Therefore materials which trap air inside them, such as cork, polystyrene and wool, are good insulators. Insulating materials have a variety of uses. Wrapping an object with insulation can keep heat in or out. Fibre-glass and polystyrene are used for loft insulation. Woollen clothing prevents heat leaving the human body.

## Convection

The most efficient way of transferring heat in liquids and gases is by convection. Convection is the upward movement of a warm liquid or gas. When a liquid (or gas) is heated, the part nearest the heat source expands, becomes less dense and rises. The cooler, denser liquid then sinks towards the heat source. The upward currents of hot liquid or gas are called **convection currents**. Some water heating systems work on the principle of convection. Water rises to the hot water tank when it is hot, and sinks to the boiler when it cools.

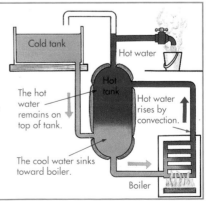

Cold tank

Hot water

Hot tank

The hot water remains on top of tank.

Hot water rises by convection.

The cool water sinks toward boiler.

Boiler

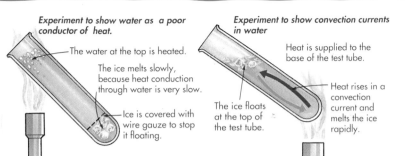

**Experiment to show water as a poor conductor of heat.**

The water at the top is heated.

The ice melts slowly, because heat conduction through water is very slow.

Ice is covered with wire gauze to stop it floating.

**Experiment to show convection currents in water**

Heat is supplied to the base of the test tube.

The ice floats at the top of the test tube.

Heat rises in a convection current and melts the ice rapidly.

## Radiation

Radiation is the method by which heat is transferred through empty spaces. Warm objects emit heat waves which can travel through a *vacuum\**. These waves are called *infra-red waves\**, and are part of the *electromagnetic spectrum\**. Infra-red waves travel away from their source at the speed of light, until they hit an object in their path. The object absorbs the heat energy and its temperature rises. The surfaces of some objects absorb more heat than others. Darkly coloured, dull surfaces absorb more radiation than shiny or light coloured ones. This is because shiny, light objects reflect back more heat energy than they absorb.

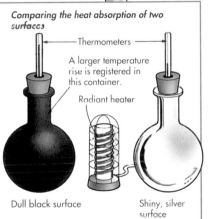

*Comparing the heat absorption of two surfaces*

Thermometers

A larger temperature rise is registered in this container.

Radiant heater

Dull black surface

Shiny, silver surface

## The greenhouse effect

A greenhouse traps the Sun's heat. High energy, short wavelength radiation from the Sun passes through its glass. The radiation is absorbed by the plants and soil inside, which in turn emit their own radiation. The radiation they emit is low energy, long wavelength, which is unable to pass through the glass and is reflected back into the greenhouse.

The warming effect produced when radiation cannot escape the atmosphere is called the **greenhouse effect**. It is caused when carbon dioxide in the atmosphere forms an insulating layer around the Earth and behaves like the glass in a greenhouse. Industrial pollution is constantly adding to carbon dioxide levels. If this continues, experts predict an increase in global temperatures, which may have a damaging effect on agriculture and human livelihood.

## A vacuum flask

A vacuum flask is designed to reduce heat transfer in any form. It is made of glass, which is a bad conductor of heat. A vacuum surrounding the liquid eliminates convection and conduction. A shiny, silvered inside surface minimizes radiation by reflecting the heat energy back into the flask.

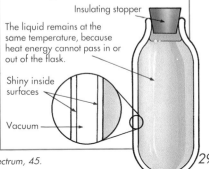

Insulating stopper

The liquid remains at the same temperature, because heat energy cannot pass in or out of the flask.

Shiny inside surfaces

Vacuum

*Vacuum 61; Infra-red waves, Electromagnetic spectrum, 45.

# Changes in state

The physical state of a substance can change if heat is added or removed from it. For example, if water is supplied with enough heat it will change to steam. If water is made cold enough it changes to ice. Changes in state are caused by the *molecules** in a substance gaining or losing their *kinetic energy**.

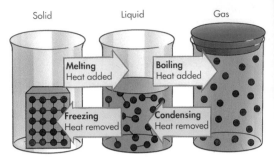

Solid     Liquid     Gas

**Melting** Heat added
**Boiling** Heat added
**Freezing** Heat removed
**Condensing** Heat removed

## Melting and boiling

The change from a solid to a liquid is called **melting**. When a substance melts, its molecules use the kinetic energy they gain from the heat source to break the forces which hold them in a solid form. The change from a liquid to a gas is called **boiling**. The molecules of the liquid use heat energy to escape the attractive forces of other molecules and move independently and freely as a gas.

## Freezing and condensing

The change from a gas to a liquid is called **condensing** and the change from a liquid to a solid is called **freezing**. These changes in state are the reverse processes of melting and boiling. Condensing and freezing involve the removal of heat energy. As a substance freezes or condenses, its molecules lose kinetic energy and reform their bonds with neighbouring molecules.

## Latent heat

While a substance is changing state its temperature does not change. For example, when water begins to boil its temperature remains constant even though heating continues. The heat supplied is used to enable the water molecules to escape the attractive forces of their neighbours. This heat is called **latent heat**.

No temperature change is observed at the condensing and freezing points of a substance. In the process of reforming

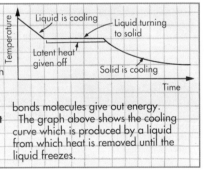

Liquid is cooling
Liquid turning to solid
Latent heat given off
Solid is cooling
Temperature
Time

bonds molecules give out energy. The graph above shows the cooling curve which is produced by a liquid from which heat is removed until the liquid freezes.

## Evaporation

When a liquid changes into a *vapour** it is said to have **evaporated**. Some of the molecules in a liquid have greater energy than others and manage to escape from the surface of the liquid, even when the

The energetic molecules escape, carrying away heat energy.

Vapour

The slower molecules remain in the liquid.

Liquid

The average energy of molecules left is lower.

liquid is not boiling. The average kinetic energy of the molecules left in the liquid is then lower. This means the temperature of the liquid has become lower. This process is called cooling by evaporation.

When human beings sweat, they produce water which evaporates from the surface of their skin. Energy is needed to give the water molecules enough energy to change into a vapour. The molecules absorb heat energy from the skin. This has the effect of cooling the body down.

*Molecule, 4; Kinetic energy, 13; Vapour, 61.

# Electricity

Electricity is the phenomenon caused by the production of electrically charged particles. There are two types of charged particle: positive and negative. These charged particles are called **ions**. Ions are produced when an electrically neutral atom loses or gains *electrons** in a process called **ionization**. An object which has a surplus of electrons is said to be **negatively charged** and an object which has a deficiency of electrons is **positively charged**. The magnitude of the electric charge on an object is measured in **coulombs** (**C**).

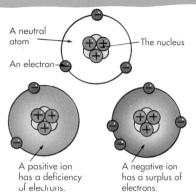

A neutral atom
The nucleus
An electron

A positive ion has a deficiency of electrons.

A negative ion has a surplus of electrons.

## Static electricity

An object is said to be charged with **static electricity** if electrically charged particles are 'held' on its surface. The charges are unable to move through the material of which the object is made. There are many everyday examples of the effects of static electricity, such as the tiny electric shock produced by touching a metal object after walking across a nylon carpet, or the way in which dust clings to a record.

Charged objects exert an **electrical force**. **Objects which carry like charges repel each other. Objects which carry opposite charges attract each other**.

## Conductors and insulators

Most materials fall into two groups: conductors and insulators. **Conductors** allow electric charges to move through them. The atoms of metals have some electrons which are free to move through the material. Metals such as silver and copper have a large number of these 'free' electrons and are very good conductors of electricity. **Insulators** are materials, such as acetate and polythene, which do not allow charges to flow through them. They hold the electric charge on their surface.

## Charging objects

The two main ways of producing electric charge are by **friction** and **induction**. If a plastic pen is rubbed with a cloth, the friction causes a transfer of charge between the pen and the cloth. Both the pen and cloth are insulators and hold the charge on their surface. When charged, the pen will attract small pieces of paper.

Static charge can be induced on a conductor by bringing a charged object close to it, but without the two touching.

The electrons are repelled by a negatively charged rod.

The metal sphere is a conductor and allows charges to move through it.

Insulator

The electrons flow away through the experimenter's body. This process is called *earthing**.

The finger is removed, and then the rod is taken away. The positive charges spread out.

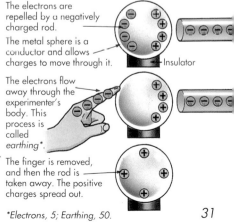

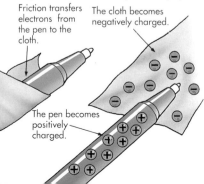

Friction transfers electrons from the pen to the cloth.

The cloth becomes negatively charged.

The pen becomes positively charged.

*Electrons, 5; Earthing, 50.

31

# Current electricity

**Electricity** is a form of energy which can be converted into different forms of energy, such as heat, light and mechanical energy. It has a wide variety of uses ranging from light bulbs and calculators to high speed trains.

An electric current is a flow of electrically charged particles. In wires this current is a stream of electrons. The size of a current depends on the rate at which electric charges flow through a conductor. It is calculated with the following equation:

$$\text{Current (I)} = \frac{\text{charge (Q)}}{\text{time (t)}}$$

Electric current is measured in **amperes** (**A**). One ampere is equal to one coulomb* of charge passing any point in the conductor in one second.

## Electric circuits

To maintain the flow of a current, a continuous conducting path is needed, called a **circuit**. A break in a circuit stops current flowing. Circuits contain components, such as lamps and ammeters (see opposite). Components convert the electrical energy carried by a current into other forms of energy, such as light and heat. They do not use up the current itself. The size of the current at the end of the circuit is the same as at the beginning.

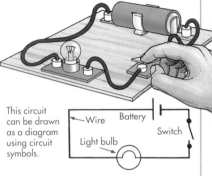

This circuit can be drawn as a diagram using circuit symbols.

## Conventional current

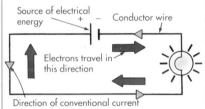

Source of electrical energy

Conductor wire

Electrons travel in this direction

Direction of conventional current

Scientists decided that current would always be shown travelling from a positively charged area to a negatively charged area. This is called **conventional current** and is indicated with an arrow on circuit diagrams. This convention was decided before it was known that the current in wires consists of electrons travelling in the opposite direction.

## Potential difference

Charged objects have *electrical potential energy\**. The amount of potential energy they have depends on the size of their charge. When there is a difference in the electrical potential energy between two areas, a current will flow if a conducting path is placed between them. Energy is carried from an area of higher electrical potential to an area of lower electrical potential. A **potential difference** (**p.d.**) is said to exist between the two areas.

Potential difference is measured in **volts** (**V**) and is often called **voltage**. The p.d. between the ends of a conductor is equal to the amount of electrical energy (in joules) which is converted into different forms for every coulomb of electric charge which passes through the conductor. P.d. is calculated with the following equation:

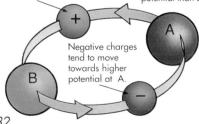

Positive charges move toward lower potential. This is the conventional current direction.

A has a higher potential than B.

Negative charges tend to move towards higher potential at A.

$$\text{Potential difference (V)} = \frac{\text{electrical energy (E)}}{\text{charge (Q)}}$$

*Coulomb, 31; Electrical potential energy, 13.

## Creating a potential difference

A potential difference is produced by an electrical energy source. An electric cell is a source of electrical energy. It contains two metal terminals. Chemical reactions in the cell give one terminal a higher electrical potential than the other. When the terminals are joined by a conductor a current will flow. The size of the p.d. between the ends of the conductor can be increased by increasing the number of cells included in a circuit. A number of cells joined together is called a **battery**.

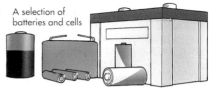
A selection of batteries and cells

## Electromotive force

An **electromotive force** (**e.m.f.**) is the energy which a cell or *dynamo*\* produces to get electric charges moving. It is a source of electrical energy because it maintains a p.d. between two terminals. An e.m.f. is measured in volts (V).

## Series and parallel circuits

Components can be arranged in a circuit in two ways: in series and in parallel. A **series** circuit has a single path for the current. The current passes through components one after another. The voltage across the cell in the circuit equals the sum of the voltages across each of the components. One disadvantage of a series circuit is that if one component stops working it breaks the circuit and the current will not flow.

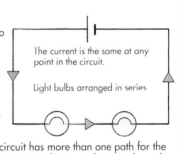
The current is the same at any point in the circuit.

Light bulbs arranged in series

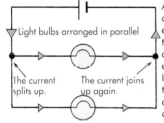
Light bulbs arranged in parallel

The current splits up. The current joins up again.

A **parallel** circuit has more than one path for the current. The current splits up and passes through each branch at once. The voltage across each of the components is equal, and equal to the voltage across the cell. The total current in the circuit is equal to the sum of the currents in all its branches. In the circuit shown, the total current is the sum of the current through both bulbs. If a component in one branch of a parallel circuit breaks, the current continues to flow through the other branches.

## Ammeters and voltmeters

An **ammeter** is a device used to measure the amount of electric current flowing through a particular point in a circuit. An ammeter must be connected in series at the point in the circuit where the current is to be measured.

A **voltmeter** is a device which is used to measure the potential difference between any two points in a circuit. It must be connected in parallel across these points. To measure the potential difference across a circuit component, a voltmeter must be connected in parallel across the component, as shown below.

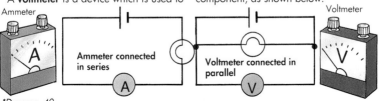
Ammeter

Ammeter connected in series

Voltmeter connected in parallel

Voltmeter

*Dynamo, 40.

## Controlling current

It is important to be able to control the amount of current flowing through a circuit. The size of the current flowing through a component can be controlled by varying the *potential difference** across the component. The current is also affected by the type of components in the circuit. Different components use different amounts of electrical energy provided by the energy source. Some components can be used to limit the current flowing through parts of a circuit.

### Current and potential difference

A current will flow through a component only if there is a potential difference across it. The size of the potential difference directly affects the amount of current which will flow.

The circuit shown below can be used to demonstrate the relationship between current and p.d. The current in the circuit and the p.d. across the component is recorded. The p.d. is then increased by adding batteries into the circuit one by one. The current is recorded each time.

The experiment shows that, for the circuit and the particular component shown, the current is directly proportional to the potential difference. This means that when the potential difference in the circuit is doubled, the current doubles. When the p.d. is trebled, the current trebles.

If the results of the experiment are plotted on a graph showing current against voltage, the gradient produced is a straight line.

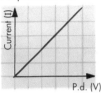

P.d. (V)

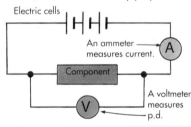

Electric cells

An ammeter measures current.

Component

A voltmeter measures p.d.

### Ohm's law

Ohm's law states that **the current flowing through a conductor is directly proportional to the p.d. across its ends, provided the temperature remains constant.**

The p.d. across a conductor divided by the current through it produces a quantity called the conductor's **resistance**. If the conductor obeys Ohm's law, this ratio always gives a constant value.

### Resistance

Resistance is the ability of a substance to resist, or oppose, the flow of an electric current in a conductor. All the components in a circuit have a certain resistance to current. This resistance makes the electrons in the current flowing through the component give up some of the electrical energy they carry. If the component is a lamp, for example, it converts the electrical energy into heat and light energy. The element in a kettle is a resistor which converts electrical energy into heat energy.

A conductor's resistance decreases if the area of its cross-section is increased. Its resistance increases if its length increases.

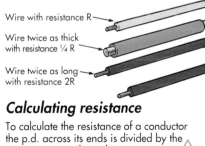

Wire with resistance R

Wire twice as thick with resistance ¼ R

Wire twice as long with resistance 2R

### Calculating resistance

To calculate the resistance of a conductor the p.d. across its ends is divided by the current passing through it.

**Resistance (R) = <u>p.d. (V)</u>**
        **current (I)**

Resistance is measured in **ohms** (Ω). One ohm is the resistance of a conductor through which a current of 1 amp passes when the p.d. between its ends is 1 volt.

*Potential difference, 32.*

## Non-ohmic conductors

Conductors which obey Ohm's law are called **ohmic**. Some conductors, such as a filament bulb, do not obey Ohm's law. These are called **non-ohmic**. The resistance of the bulb's tungsten filament increases as its temperature increases. It produces a current/voltage graph like the one shown. A *thermistor* is also made of non-ohmic material. Its resistance decreases as its temperature increases.

Current (I) — Filament bulb

P.d. (V)
The current/voltage graph for a filament bulb.

## Resistors

**Resistors** control the current flowing in a circuit. When included in a circuit, resistors limit the current passing through components, reducing the danger of damage caused by over-heating.

There are two main types of resistor: **fixed resistors** and **variable resistors**. Fixed resistors are available at different resistance values. Variable resistors are called **rheostats**. By adjusting a rheostat the amount of current flowing through a circuit can be controlled. A device called a **potential divider** (or voltage divider) can be used in a circuit to produce a required p.d. from another higher p.d. A potential divider divides the voltage

supplied by the battery, enabling different sized currents to flow through different parts of a circuit.

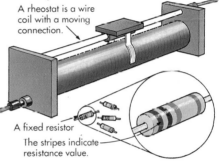

A rheostat is a wire coil with a moving connection.

A fixed resistor

The stripes indicate resistance value.

## Resistors in series

If the resistors in a circuit are arranged *in series** the total resistance in the circuit is equal to the sum of the resistance of all the resistors. This is written:

**Total circuit resistance (R) = $R_1 + R_2 + R_3$**

For example, the total resistance in the circuit below is calculated:

Total resistance (R) = 3 + 5 + 2
= 10 ohms

The magnitude of the current in this circuit is calculated using Ohm's law:

$$\text{Current (I)} = \frac{\text{p.d. (V)}}{\text{resistance (R)}}$$
$$= \frac{20}{10}$$
$$= 2 \text{ amps}$$

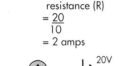

R₁ (3 Ω)    R₂ (5 Ω)    R₃ (2 Ω)    20V

## Resistors in parallel

The total resistance in a circuit where the resistors are arranged *in parallel** is calculated with the equation:

$$\frac{1}{R} = \frac{1}{R_1} + \frac{1}{R_2} + \frac{1}{R_3}$$

For example, the total resistance in the circuit below is calculated:

$$\frac{1}{R} = \frac{1}{6} + \frac{1}{12} + \frac{1}{4} = \frac{6}{12}$$
$$R = \frac{12}{6} = 2 \text{ ohms}$$

The total current in the circuit is calculated:

$$I = \frac{V}{R} = \frac{20}{2} = 10 \text{ amps}$$

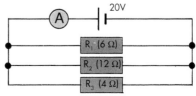

20V
R₁ (6 Ω)
R₂ (12 Ω)
R₃ (4 Ω)

*Thermistor, 46; Series , Parallel, 33.

# Magnetism

The ability to attract iron and steel is called **magnetism** and materials which have this property are called **magnetic**. Knowledge of magnetism goes back to the Ancient Greeks who realized that a rock called magnetite attracted pieces of iron. If a bar magnet is hung by a thread, it will rotate until it is pointing in a north-south direction. The regions near the ends of a magnet are called its **poles**.

The end which points south is called the **south pole**.

The end which points north is called the **north pole**.

## Repulsion and attraction

If two north or two south poles are brought towards each other, they will push away, or repel, each other.

If one north pole and one south pole of two magnets are brought together, they will pull towards, or attract, each other.

## The law of magnetism

The behaviour of the *magnetic forces** exerted by the two bar magnets shown demonstrates the law of magnetism. This law states that **the like poles of two magnets repel each other, and the unlike poles attract each other.**

## Magnetic materials

If materials such as cobalt, nickel or iron are put near a magnet they begin to act like magnets. This is called **magnetic induction**. Materials which react in this way are called **ferromagnetic**.

Iron is a 'soft' ferromagnetic material. This means it will become magnetized very easily, but quickly loses its magnetic properties if the magnetizing force is removed. Steel is more difficult to magnetize, but once it is magnetized, it retains its magnetic properties for a long time. Steel is called a 'hard' ferromagnetic material.

## How to make a magnet

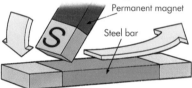

Permanent magnet

Steel bar

A steel bar will become magnetized if it is stroked repeatedly with one pole of a permanent magnet. The magnet should be lifted high above the bar between each stroke. This '**single touch**' method produces a weak magnet.

## What happens when something is magnetized.

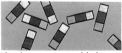

The domains are jumbled in a non-magnetized state

The domains line up in a magnetized state

In magnetic materials there are groups of *molecules**, called **domains**, which behave like tiny magnets. When a piece of magnetic material is in a non-magnetized state, these domains are jumbled up. When it is magnetized, the domains line up, with all their north poles pointing north and their south poles pointing south. Most materials (including some metals) cannot be magnetized. This is because the molecules in these substances do not behave like domains.

Magnetism can be destroyed by extreme heat. Heat makes the domains in a magnetized material vibrate and break out of their ordered pattern. They return to a jumbled, non-magnetized state.

*Magnetic force, 8; Molecules, 4.

## Magnetic fields

A magnet is surrounded by an area called its **magnetic field**. Magnetic objects entering this field are affected by the magnet's forces of attraction and repulsion. The pattern of a magnetic field can be plotted on a sheet of paper using a plotting compass. The position of the compass's needle is marked as shown in the diagram. The north pole of the compass is attracted toward the south pole of the magnet.

The strength and direction of a magnetic field is shown by **magnetic field lines** (sometimes called **magnetic flux lines**). These lines have arrows which indicate the direction in which a plotting compass's north pole would point if placed in the field. Magnetic force is strongest near a magnet's poles, and so the magnetic field lines are drawn very close together.

If the like poles of two magnets are

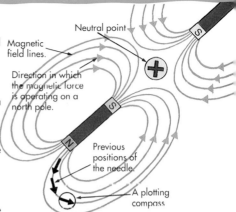

Neutral point

Magnetic field lines.

Direction in which the magnetic force is operating on a north pole.

Previous positions of the needle.

A plotting compass

placed close together, as shown in the diagram, their magnetic fields combine to produce **neutral points**. These are areas where the magnetic forces are equal but opposite and cancel each other out.

## Creating a permanent magnet with a solenoid

The most efficient and effective way of creating magnets is by an electrical method using a *solenoid coil*\*. An electric current flowing through the wire coil of a solenoid produces a magnetic field which is similar in shape to that produced by a bar magnet. If a bar of ferromagnetic material is placed inside the solenoid, the magnetic force makes the domains in the metal line up in a north-south direction, and the bar begins to act like a magnet.

To create a permanent magnet, a strong magnetic force is needed. The solenoid

must have a large number of turns of wire per unit length and must be supplied with a large *direct current*\*. A steel bar placed in this magnetic field will become magnetized, retaining its magnetism even when the current is switched off.

The position of the new magnet's poles depends on the direction of the current in the solenoid. The memory aid below is a useful means of working out which end of the magnet is a north pole and which end a south pole. These will be reversed if the current direction is reversed.

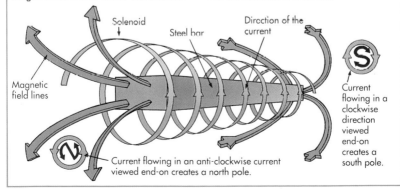

Solenoid

Steel bar

Direction of the current

Magnetic field lines

Current flowing in a clockwise direction viewed end-on creates a south pole.

Current flowing in an anti-clockwise current viewed end-on creates a north pole.

*Solenoid coil, 38; Direct current, 40.

# Electromagnetism

When an electric current flows in a conductor it produces a *magnetic field*\*. This effect is called **electromagnetism**. The field is circular and can be plotted with a small compass. The direction of the magnetic field around a wire depends on the direction the current is flowing through the wire. The **right-hand grip rule** (shown in the diagram), is a useful method of working out the direction of the field. If the right hand is held as if gripping the wire, with the thumb pointing in the direction of the current, the fingers are pointing in the direction of the magnetic field lines.

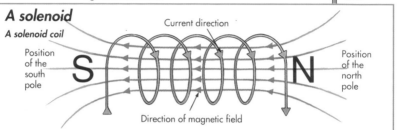

The thumb points in the direction of the current.

The fingers point in the direction of the magnetic field.

Right hand

Magnetic field

Plotting compass

◄Wire

## A solenoid

**A solenoid coil**

Current direction

Position of the south pole

S

N

Position of the north pole

Direction of magnetic field

A **solenoid** is a cylindrical coil of insulated wire. When a current flows through it, the magnetic fields produced by each part of the wire combine to produce a strong magnetic force inside the solenoid. The shape of the field outside the coil is like that of a *bar magnet*\*. The position of the poles can be found using the memory aid shown on page 37. The strength of the magnetic field in the solenoid will increase if the size of the current increases, or if the length of the wire on the solenoid is increased, by wrapping it more closely along the length of the solenoid.

## Electromagnets

The electromagnetic effect is used to make powerful magnets called **electromagnets**. If a piece of 'soft' iron\* is placed inside a solenoid coil and the current is switched on, the iron becomes magnetized. The combined magnetism of the solenoid and the magnetized iron core is very strong. 'Soft' iron is used because it only acts as a magnet when the current is on. So the magnetism of an electromagnet can be switched on and off with the current. Electromagnets which are the shape of the one shown here, with unlike poles next to each other, produce a very strong magnetic field.

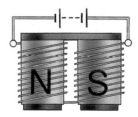

N S

An electromagnet formed from two solenoids with iron cores.

## A relay switch

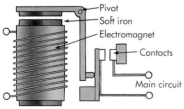

Pivot
Soft iron
Electromagnet
Contacts
Main circuit

When electromagnets are switched on they attract *ferromagnetic*\* materials towards them. For example, in a **relay** switch, an electromagnet operated by a small current is used to close a pair of metal contacts, which completes a main circuit. This means that a small current in the electromagnet's coil can switch on a large current without the circuits being electrically linked.

*Magnetic field, Bar magnet, Soft iron, Ferromagnetic, 36.

## The motor effect

When a current-carrying wire is brought into a magnetic field, a force acts on it producing an effect called the **motor effect**. The wire may be thrust out of the magnet's field. The motion of the wire is always at right angles to both the magnetic field and the current direction. If there is an increase in the size of the current through the wire, or the strength of the magnetic field, the motor effect becomes stronger.

The direction of the motor effect can be worked out using **Fleming's left-hand rule**, which is a useful memory aid. The thumb and first two fingers of the left hand are held at right angles to each other, as shown in the diagram. If the first finger points in the direction of the magnetic field and the second finger points in the direction of the current, the thumb will be pointing in the direction of the thrust force or the motor effect.

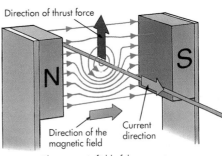

Direction of thrust force

Direction of the magnetic field

Current direction

The magnetic field of the current and the magnet combine below the wire, producing an upward force.

The **Th**umb will point in the direction of the **Th**rust force.

The **F**irst finger points in the direction of the magnetic **F**ield.

The se**C**ond finger points in the direction the **C**urrent is flowing.

## A simple d.c. electric motor

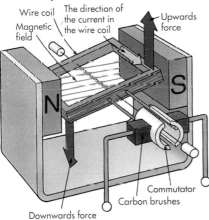

Wire coil

Magnetic field

The direction of the current in the wire coil

Upwards force

Commutator

Carbon brushes

Downwards force

A **simple *direct current*\* electric motor** uses the motor effect to convert electrical energy into *kinetic energy*\*. A flat coil of current-carrying wire is placed in a magnetic field. One side of the wire coil experiences an upwards force, while the other side experiences a downward force. This makes the coil rotate until it is vertical. At this point the coil stops moving, unless the direction of the current through the coil is reversed. A **commutator**, formed of a metal ring split into two halves, is used to reverse the current direction in the coil every half turn, making the motion of the coil continuous. The current enters and leaves the commutator through two carbon brushes.

## A galvanometer

**Galvanometers** measure electric current. They contain a moving coil which turns when a current flows through it. The greater the current, the more the coil turns, tightening a return spring. This moves a pointer across a scale, indicating the size of the current.

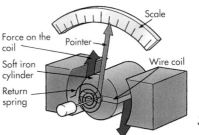

Scale

Force on the coil

Pointer

Soft iron cylinder

Wire coil

Return spring

*\*Direct current, 40; Kinetic energy, 13.*

# Electromagnetic induction

If a conductor wire is moved in a magnetic field so that it cuts through the magnetic field lines, an **electromotive force (e.m.f.)** is induced in the wire. If the wire forms a circuit, the e.m.f. causes a current to flow. This effect is called **electromagnetic induction.** It happens whenever a conductor cuts through magnetic field lines or if it is placed in a changing magnetic field.

The size of the e.m.f. induced in the wire is affected by three factors: the length of wire moving in the magnetic field; the speed of the wire's movement; and the strength of the magnetic field. If any of these three quantities is increased, the size of the e.m.f. induced in the wire increases.

The current only flows while the wire is cutting through magnetic field lines. The maximum e.m.f. is produced when the wire's movement is at right angles to field lines. When the wire is stationary or moving parallel to the field lines without cutting them, the current does not flow.

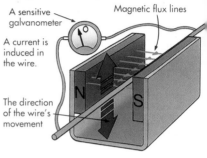

A sensitive galvanometer

Magnetic flux lines

A current is induced in the wire.

The direction of the wire's movement

N          S

## Simple dynamos

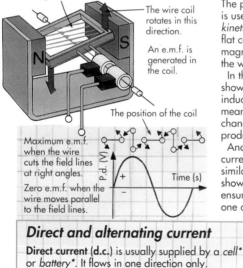

Magnetic field

The wire coil rotates in this direction.

An e.m.f. is generated in the coil.

N          S

The position of the coil

Maximum e.m.f. when the wire cuts the field lines at right angles.

Zero e.m.f. when the wire moves parallel to the field lines.

P.d. (V)

Time (s)

The principle of electromagnetic induction is used in a **simple dynamo** to convert *kinetic energy** into electrical energy. A flat coil of conducting wire is rotated in a magnetic field. This induces an e.m.f. in the wire and a current flows.

In the alternating current dynamo, shown here, an alternating e.m.f. is induced in the coil as it rotates. This means the direction of the induced e.m.f. changes at regular intervals, which produces an alternating current in the coil.

Another simple dynamo called the direct current dynamo has a commutator, similar to the one on the electric motor shown on page 39. The commutator rings ensure that the current always flows in one direction only.

## Direct and alternating current

**Direct current (d.c.)** is usually supplied by a *cell** or *battery**. It flows in one direction only.

The electricity which is supplied to houses by power stations is called **alternating current (a.c.).** The direction of this current changes many times a second. This means the electrons in the current flow alternately one way and then the other, as the ends of the circuit change rapidly from positive to negative and back again.

If d.c. and a.c. voltages are displayed on the screen of a *cathode ray oscilloscope** they produce the voltage/time graphs shown here.

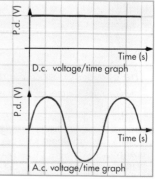

P.d. (V)

Time (s)

D.c. voltage/time graph

P.d. (V)

Time (s)

A.c. voltage/time graph

*Kinetic energy, 13; Cell, Battery, 33; Cathode ray oscilloscope, 48.

## Transformers

**Transformers** are used to change the size of a voltage. A transformer consists of two coils of wire wound on to a soft iron core. An alternating voltage is supplied to one coil (the primary coil). The changing direction of the alternating current produces an alternating magnetic field in the iron core. This has the same effect on the other coil (the secondary coil) as moving a wire through a magnetic field. The changing magnetic field induces a voltage in the secondary coil. Therefore, by using a transformer, electrical energy can be transferred from the primary coil to the secondary coil without the coils being electrically connected.

The size of the voltage induced in the secondary coil depends on the size of the voltage applied to the primary coil.

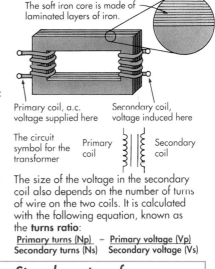

The soft iron core is made of laminated layers of iron.

Primary coil, a.c. voltage supplied here

Secondary coil, voltage induced here

The circuit symbol for the transformer

Primary coil

Secondary coil

The size of the voltage in the secondary coil also depends on the number of turns of wire on the two coils. It is calculated with the following equation, known as the **turns ratio**:

$$\frac{\text{Primary turns (Np)}}{\text{Secondary turns (Ns)}} = \frac{\text{Primary voltage (Vp)}}{\text{Secondary voltage (Vs)}}$$

## Step-up transformers

A **step-up transformer** is one in which the number of turns of wire on the secondary coil is larger than those on the primary coil. When a voltage is applied to a primary coil, a voltage of greater magnitude is produced in the secondary coil. As the number of turns of wire on the secondary coil increases, the total voltage produced increases. Step-up transformers are used to produce the high voltage at which electricity is transmitted by the *grid system**.

*Step-up transformer*

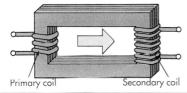

Primary coil          Secondary coil

## Step-down transformers

A **step-down transformer** is one in which the number of turns of wire on the secondary coil is smaller than those on the primary coil. When a voltage is applied to the primary coil, a voltage of smaller magnitude is produced in the secondary coil. Many electrical appliances require a voltage much lower than that supplied by the grid system. These appliances often contain step-down transformers to change, or transform, the mains voltage to the lower voltages they require.

*Step-down transformer*

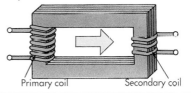

Primary coil          Secondary coil

## The efficiency of a transformer

Transformers are very efficient devices. Two circuits linked by a well-designed transformer lose very little electrical energy. A current flowing through a material produces heat which wastes energy. Therefore, low resistance copper wire is used on a transformer to minimize the amount of heat produced. The iron core of a transformer is made of varnished sheets of iron, which have been glued together. These insulated sheets reduce the waste of energy in the form of heat by minimizing the currents induced in the core by electromagnetic induction.

*Grid system, 50.

# Radioactivity

Some substances, like uranium and radium, are **radioactive**. This means the nuclei of their atoms are unstable. They break up, and emit particles or rays known as **radiation**. This process is called **radioactive decay**. Some substances only emit radiation in controlled conditions.

Some atoms belonging to the same element have a different number of neutrons in their nucleus. These atoms are called **isotopes**. All the isotopes of a particular element have the same *proton*

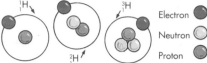

*Three isotopes of hydrogen*

Electron
Neutron
Proton

*number\**, but a different *nucleon number\** Some atoms have a much larger number of neutrons than protons in their nuclei. It is thought that this causes atoms to be unstable and prone to radioactive decay.

## Radiation

Three types of radiation can be emitted by radioactive materials: alpha ($\alpha$) particles, beta ($\beta$) particles and gamma ($\gamma$) rays. When a nucleus decays, energy is released. If alpha or beta particles are

emitted, a new nucleus is formed. This change in a nucleus can be written as an equation. The equations vary according to the type of radiation emitted and some examples are shown below.

## Alpha particles

An **alpha particle** is a helium nucleus, which consist of two protons and two neutrons. It is emitted from an atom's nucleus in a process called **alpha decay**. The diagram shows alpha decay taking place. If a thorium–232 nucleus undergoes alpha decay, its original proton number is reduced by two and its nucleon number is reduced by four. This can be written: $^{232}_{90}\text{Th} \longrightarrow {}^{228}_{88}\text{Ra} + {}^{4}_{2}\text{He}$

*Alpha decay*

Radium–228 nucleus

Thorium–232 nucleus

Alpha particle

## Beta particles

*Beta decay*

Polonium–212 nucleus

Bismuth–212 nucleus

Beta particle

A **beta particle** is an electron formed in an atom's nucleus when a neutron decays, splitting into a proton and an electron. The electron is emitted in a process called **beta decay**. The diagram shows beta decay. If a bismuth–212 nucleus undergoes beta decay, its original proton number increases by one. Its nucleon number remains the same, because a neutron has formed a proton. This is written: $^{212}_{83}\text{Bi} \longrightarrow {}^{212}_{84}\text{Po} + {}^{0}_{-1}\text{e}$

## Gamma rays

After an atom has undergone alpha or beta decay, it may be left with excess energy. The atom becomes more stable by emitting this excess energy in the form of gamma radiation. Gamma rays are part of the *electromagnetic spectrum\**. The rays are not particles, so the atom's nucleon and proton number remain unchanged. This is written: $^{228}_{88}\text{Ra} \longrightarrow {}^{228}_{88}\text{Ra} + \gamma$

*Gamma radiation*

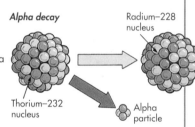

Gamma rays

Radium–228 nucleus

## Ionization

Alpha particles, beta particles and gamma rays *ionize** the substances through which they pass. However, producing ions reduces the energy of the radiation. Alpha particles cause a great deal of ionization, which quickly reduces their energy and limits the distance they can travel. Beta particles are more penetrating because they cause less ionization. Gamma rays travel the greatest distance because they cause only minimal ionization in the substances through which they pass.

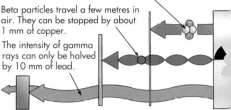

Alpha particles travel a few centimetres in air. They can be stopped by a sheet of paper.

Beta particles travel a few metres in air. They can be stopped by about 1 mm of copper.

The intensity of gamma rays can only be halved by 10 mm of lead.

## A Geiger counter

A **Geiger counter** is used to detect radioactivity. It consists of a **Geiger–Müller tube**, a **scaler** and/or a **ratemeter**. Radiation produces ionization in the gas-filled tube. This causes electrical pulses to pass between the positively charged central wire and the negatively charged metal wall. The scaler then counts each of the pulses and the ratemeter measures the average rate of pulses in counts per second. A high **count-rate** indicates a high level of ionizing radiation in the test sample. The tube can also be connected to an amplifier and loudspeaker, so that a click is heard every time a pulse passes between the wire and the wall.

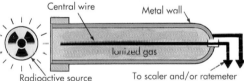

Central wire

Metal wall

Ionized gas

Radioactive source

To scaler and/or ratemeter

## Background radiation

**Background radiation** is the radiation which is continually present on Earth. It has a variety of sources including the following: radioactive materials in the Earth; cosmic radiation from outer space; radioactive waste (from both the nuclear power industry and the use of radioactive isotopes in medicine - see page 44); and the nuclear weapons industry. There are even some radioactive elements which occur naturally in the human body. Background radiation can easily be measured with a Geiger counter, which produces a **background count**.

## Radioactive half-life

The process of radioactive decay is completely random. This means it is impossible to say when any particular atom of a radioactive sample will decay. Physicists can measure how long it takes, on average, for the radioactivity of a test sample to fall by half. This is called a **half-life**. Each type of isotope has a different half-life. It varies from a fraction of a second to millions of years.

If the count-rate of an isotope is plotted against time, a graph is produced. It can be used to calculate an isotope's half-life and predict the count-rate of a sample at any given moment.

The graph below shows the decreasing count-rate of a substance whose half-life is ten seconds. This means that for every ten second period that passes the count-rate of the sample will be halved.

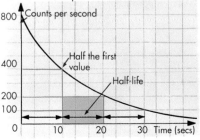

Counts per second

800

Half the first value

400

Half-life

200

100

0    10    20    30   Time (secs)

# Using radiation and nuclear energy

The radiation emitted by some isotopes can be put to a variety of uses in medicine and industry.

**Radiocarbon dating** is a method used by archaeologists to calculate the age of preserved, organic materials such as leather, parchment or textiles. All living things contain carbon–14 which emits radiation. After death, carbon–14 is not replenished and its emission decreases. The age of remains can be calculated from the strength of the emission, using carbon–14's half-life (6,000 years).

**Radiotherapy** is the use of carefully controlled doses of high level radiation to destroy cancerous cells.

**Radioactive tracing** uses the movement and concentration of radioactive isotopes in the body to study the functions of organs and to diagnose disorders. For example, radioactive iodine is used to study the thyroid gland. A high concentration of the isotope in the gland may indicate the presence of cancer.

**Radiography** is used in industrial quality control. Faults in materials can be detected using a beta radiation source and a Geiger counter. For example, to ensure a roll of paper is of even thickness, a scalar is used to alert machine operators. When the count-rate goes down the paper is too thick; if it goes up the paper is too thin.

## Radioactivity and safety

Exposure to radiation must be minimized because it can seriously damage living cells. In laboratories and schools radioactive sources are stored in lead containers. When in use they are handled with forceps and kept at a distance from people behind lead shields. In nuclear power stations, people working with larger radioactive sources must wear special clothing and devices.

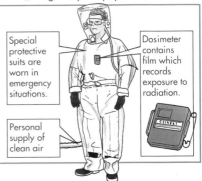

Special protective suits are worn in emergency situations.

Personal supply of clean air

Dosimeter contains film which records exposure to radiation.

## The nuclear power industry

A vast amount of energy is stored in the nucleus of an atom which can be released by a process called **fission**. During this process uranium nuclei are bombarded with neutrons. They become unstable and split, releasing energy. Each nucleus also emits two or three neutrons which hit other atoms, causing more fission. This is called a **chain reaction**. An uncontrolled reaction would cause an atomic explosion. In a

nuclear *reactor**, the fission process is slowed down using control rods which absorb some of the neutrons. Fission produces heat which is used to generate electricity using steam driven *turbines**.

Nuclear power stations generate more energy per unit mass of fuel than any other type of power station. Nuclear power is clean to produce, compared with the burning of fossil fuels which causes environmental problems like the *greenhouse effect**. However, building reactors is expensive. The waste materials are radioactive, and great care must be taken when transporting and disposing of them. They are sealed in concrete and buried deep in vaults underground or dropped into the sea. The consequences of a nuclear accident are catastrophic. In 1986 an accident at Chernobyl, USSR, left many dead and vast areas of land were contaminated with radiation.

*Reactor, Turbines, 61; Greenhouse effect, 29.

*Nuclear fission causing a chain reaction*

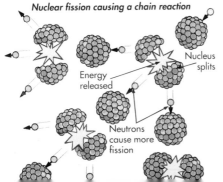

Nucleus splits

Energy released

Neutrons cause more fission

# The electromagnetic spectrum

The **electromagnetic spectrum** is made up of a huge range of energy-carrying waves called **electromagnetic waves**. The waves are produced in different ways, by different sources and have different *wavelengths** and *frequencies**. However, they do have common properties which link them. They are all *transverse waves** and are made up of oscillating electric and magnetic fields. All the waves carry energy from one place to another. They can pass through a *vacuum**, as they do not need the particles of a medium to travel. All the waves travel at the same speed (approximately 300,000,000 m/s in a vacuum). This is very much faster than the speed of sound (330 m/s). It is important to remember where each group of electromagnetic waves appears in the spectrum. In the sequence below the wavelength of the waves becomes shorter as you go down the page.

| Type | Sources | Detection | Uses | |
|---|---|---|---|---|
| Radio waves Microwaves | Electrical circuits and transmitters | Radio waves can be detected by radio aerials and television. | Radio waves are used in communication systems. Microwaves are used in radar detection and satellite communications. They are also used for cooking in microwave ovens. | |
| Infra-red radiation | Warm and hot objects | Infra-red is strongly absorbed by objects and causes a rise in temperature. | With heat-seeking equipment, hot objects can be identified at night by the infra-red radiation they emit. Infra-red sensitive cameras are used in medicine to detect disease. | |
| Visible light | Hot objects, such as fire or lamps | Light is visible to human eye and photographic film. | Apart from enabling us to see objects, light is used in optical fibres for medicine and communications. Plants need visible light to grow. | |
| Ultra-violet radiation | Very hot objects such as the Sun and mercury vapour lamps | UV rays are detected by photographic film. Fluorescent materials absorb UV rays and radiate visible light, called fluorescence. | Some washing powders use fluorescent chemicals to make washing look whiter. UV rays causes the human skin to tan. High energy UV waves can damage the cells of plants and can cause skin cancer in humans. Most UV rays from the Sun are absorbed by the *ozone layer**. If the ozone layer continues to be destroyed cases of skin cancer may increase. | |
| X-rays | X-ray tubes | X-rays are detected by special types of photographic film. | Low energy X-rays are used in medicine for studying broken bone and detecting cracks in metal objects. X-rays are harmful to living cells. Repeated exposure to X-rays can cause cancer. | |
| Gamma rays | *Radioactive** materials | Gamma rays are detected by *Geiger–Müller tubes**. | Gamma rays are used in medicine to kill cancerous growths, to kill bacteria when sterilizing instruments and to study the function of organs. Large doses of gamma rays can damage living cells. | |

*Wavelength, Frequency, Transverse waves, 16; Vacuum, Ozone layer, 61;
Radioactivity 42, Geiger–Müller tube, 43.

# Electronics

Electronics is the careful and precise control of tiny *electric currents** and *voltages**. Electronic components are built into circuits which perform specific tasks. Digital watches, calculators and computers all work by electronic means.

Electronic components are made from substances called **semiconductors** whose ability to conduct electricity lies between that of *conductors** and *insulators**.

Semiconductor materials, such as silicon, are mixed with a small amount of impurity in a process called **doping**. Depending on the type and quantity of impurity used, the semiconductor produced has different current-carrying properties.

Electronic components are used as 'switches' in circuits, because their ability to conduct electricity is affected by factors such as heat, light and current direction.

## Diodes

Diodes can be used as 'one way' switches. They allow an electric current to flow through them in one direction only. A diode is said to be '**forward biased**' when current flows through it. However, if the diode is reversed in the circuit, it will not conduct current and is said to be '**reverse biased**'. Diodes can be used to change *a.c.** to *d.c.** in a process called **rectification**. If a circuit which includes a diode is supplied by an a.c. voltage, the diode acts as a valve, because it allows the current to flow in one direction only. A diode used like this is called a **half-wave rectifier**, because half of the a.c. is cut out. A.c. which has undergone half-wave rectification will produce the time/voltage graph shown.

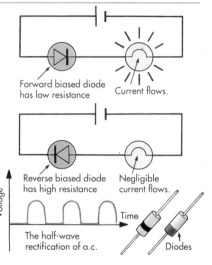

Forward biased diode has low resistance — Current flows.

Reverse biased diode has high resistance — Negligible current flows.

Voltage / Time

The half-wave rectification of a.c.

Diodes

## Light emitting diodes (LEDs)

An LED

The LED's circuit symbol

Digital displays use shaped LEDs.

**Light emitting diodes** emit light, glowing like tiny bulbs, when they are forward biased. LEDs and diodes can be damaged by large currents, so a *resistor** must be included in the circuit.

## Light dependent resistors (LDRs)

The resistance of a **light dependent resistor** depends on the amount of light it is exposed to. In the dark, its resistance is very high and it allows only a very tiny current to flow through it. However, in the light, the LDR's resistance is very low and a much larger current can flow through it. LDRs are used in alarm systems to detect light.

The LDR's circuit symbol

The LDR is sensitive to light.

## Thermistors

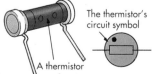

The thermistor's circuit symbol

A thermistor

A **thermistor**'s resistance depends on its temperature. When it is cold, its resistance is high. As the temperature increases its resistance decreases. Thermistors are used in fire alarm systems and thermostat systems to regulate temperature.

*Electric currents, Voltages, 32; Conductors, Insulators, 31; Resistor 35; A.c., D.c., 40.

## Transistors

A **transistor** is a component which is used as an electronic switch. It is connected into a circuit at three points called the **base**, the **collector** and the **emitter**. When a small current flows into the base, the resistance between the collector and the emitter changes from very high to very low and a current flows. Therefore, by controlling the size of the base current, the much larger collector/emitter current can be switched on and off. The voltage between base and emitter must exceed 0.6 V before the base current can switch on the collector current.

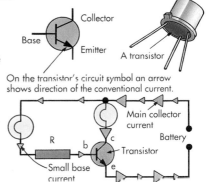

On the transistor's circuit symbol an arrow shows direction of the conventional current.

## Electronic switches

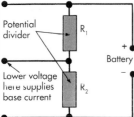

Electronic components can be combined to make switches which turn on and off in response to different conditions. In a switch circuit which includes a transistor, a *potential divider** is used to vary the voltage between the base and the emitter. Resistors $R_1$ and $R_2$ (shown in the diagram) form a potential divider. They divide the voltage supplied by the battery. This creates a lower voltage between them which can be used to supply a small base current to the transistor.

## A light sensitive switch

When light falls on the LDR in this circuit, its resistance becomes low. The p.d. between the base and emitter is very low. The transistor is switched off and no current flows between the collector and emitter. In the dark the LDR's resistance is much higher. The p.d. between the base and emitter becomes large enough for a current to flow and to switch on the transistor.

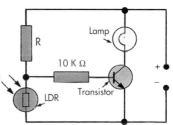

## A heat sensitive switch

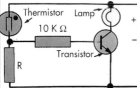

In this circuit, when the thermistor's temperature is low, its resistance is high. The p.d. between the base and the emitter is too low to switch on the transistor. When the thermistor's temperature rises, its resistance becomes low. The p.d. between the base and emitter of the transistor becomes large enough to switch the transistor on and the warning lamp light up.

## The uses of electronic devices

The miniaturization of electronic equipment and the cheap cost of components has lead to the widespread use of electronic systems - in industry, offices, schools, hospitals and communication systems. Complex circuits are built to perform particular tasks. Devices ranging from calculators to word processors contain electronic circuits.

*Potential divider, 35.

# The cathode ray oscilloscope

The **cathode ray oscilloscope (CRO)** is used to study wave *frequencies** and *waveforms**, and to measure *voltage**.

The CRO contains a **cathode ray tube** which produces a beam of electrons called a **cathode ray**. This ray hits a **fluorescent screen** and produces a spot of light. The spot is swept repeatedly across the screen at a preselected speed. This produces a trace across the screen. If a voltage signal is fed into the CRO's signal inputs, the spot's position on the screen is affected. The trace produced shows how the voltage changes with time.

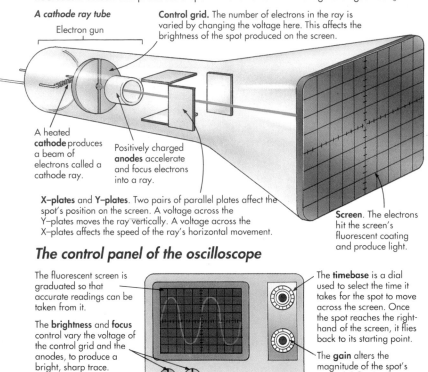

*A cathode ray tube*

Electron gun

**Control grid.** The number of electrons in the ray is varied by changing the voltage here. This affects the brightness of the spot produced on the screen.

A heated **cathode** produces a beam of electrons called a cathode ray.

Positively charged **anodes** accelerate and focus electrons into a ray.

**X–plates** and **Y–plates**. Two pairs of parallel plates affect the spot's position on the screen. A voltage across the Y–plates moves the ray vertically. A voltage across the X–plates affects the speed of the ray's horizontal movement.

**Screen**. The electrons hit the screen's fluorescent coating and produce light.

## The control panel of the oscilloscope

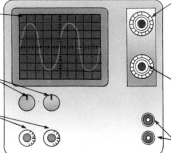

The fluorescent screen is graduated so that accurate readings can be taken from it.

The **brightness** and **focus** control vary the voltage of the control grid and the anodes, to produce a bright, sharp trace.

The **X-shift** and **Y-shift** alter the position of the spot on the screen, vertically and horizontally.

The **timebase** is a dial used to select the time it takes for the spot to move across the screen. Once the spot reaches the right-hand of the screen, it flies back to its starting point.

The **gain** alters the magnitude of the spot's vertical deflection by varying the voltage across the Y-plates.

**Signal inputs**

## Displaying waveforms on the CRO screen

When the CRO's timebase is switched on and the spot is moving across the screen at a constant speed, the screen's horizontal axis becomes a time-scale. If a voltage is then applied across the Y-plates, the trace displays a waveform which shows how the size of this voltage varies with time.

Trace produced by a 4 V a.c. voltage source.

Trace produced by a 4 V d.c. voltage source.

# Logic gates

A **logic gate** is an electronic component which can be used as a switch in a circuit. Logic gates have one or two **input** connections and one **output** connection. They are called gates because they are either 'open', which means their output is at a high *voltage**, or 'closed', which means that their output is at a low voltage. The gates can only be opened if a certain combination of information is fed into them. This information takes the form of voltages.

Voltages are applied across the inputs of a logic gate. These voltages can be either high or low. When the right combination of high and low voltages is fed into the inputs, the gate opens which means its output is high. For example, the symbol below is for a logic gate called an AND gate. The output of an AND gate (C) will only be at a high voltage when both its input voltages (A and B) are high.

*An AND gate*

Input A ————
                 ⊐D——— Output C
Input B ————

## Truth tables

There are five basic logic gates. The combinations of high and low voltages which will open these gates can be represented in the form of a **truth table**. In these truth tables high voltages are coded '1' and low voltages are coded '0'.

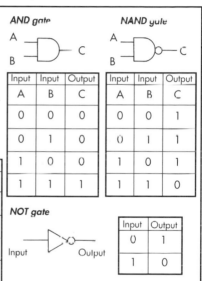

### AND gate

| Input | Input | Output |
|-------|-------|--------|
| A | B | C |
| 0 | 0 | 0 |
| 0 | 1 | 0 |
| 1 | 0 | 0 |
| 1 | 1 | 1 |

### NAND gate

| Input | Input | Output |
|-------|-------|--------|
| A | B | C |
| 0 | 0 | 1 |
| 0 | 1 | 1 |
| 1 | 0 | 1 |
| 1 | 1 | 0 |

### OR gate

| Input | Input | Output |
|-------|-------|--------|
| A | B | C |
| 0 | 0 | 0 |
| 0 | 1 | 1 |
| 1 | 0 | 1 |
| 1 | 1 | 1 |

### NOR gate

| Input | Input | Output |
|-------|-------|--------|
| A | B | C |
| 0 | 0 | 1 |
| 0 | 1 | 0 |
| 1 | 0 | 0 |
| 1 | 1 | 0 |

### NOT gate

Input ——▷o—— Output

| Input | Output |
|-------|--------|
| 0 | 1 |
| 1 | 0 |

## Combining gates

Logic gates can be linked together as shown below. A truth table can be produced to determine the final output.

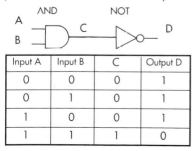

AND        NOT

A ——
      ⊐D—— C ——▷o—— D
B ——

| Input A | Input B | C | Output D |
|---------|---------|---|----------|
| 0 | 0 | 0 | 1 |
| 0 | 1 | 0 | 1 |
| 1 | 0 | 0 | 1 |
| 1 | 1 | 1 | 0 |

In most electronic devices, many logic gates are linked together to form complex circuits. These circuits can be used to perform all sorts of functions. For example, the central processing unit of a computer contains thousands of linked logic gates.

These complex circuits are called **integrated circuits** when they are put on to an electronic component called a **microchip**. Each microchip is made from a tiny slice of silicon.

# Household electricity

Electricity for domestic and industrial use is mostly produced in power stations using large *generators**. These generators are powered by the heat energy produced by burning fossil fuels, or from the heat energy produced by *nuclear fission**.

Electricity is transmitted around the country by a network of overhead cables known as a **grid system**. This grid system supplies *alternating current**. A.c. is used because *transformers**, which are used to reduce or increase *voltage**, only function if they are supplied with an alternating voltage. The electricity is transmitted at very high voltage. It is cheaper to transmit electricity at high voltage because less energy is wasted as heat in the cables.

*The grid system*

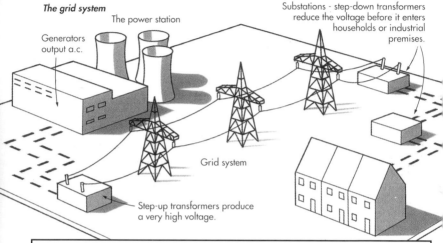

Generators output a.c.

The power station

Substations - step-down transformers reduce the voltage before it enters households or industrial premises.

Grid system

Step-up transformers produce a very high voltage.

## Electrical safety devices in the home

When an electric current flows through a wire it produces heat. If wires overheat, appliances can be damaged and fires may start. **Fuses** are fitted in circuits to reduce the possibility of overheating by limiting the size of the current which can flow through a wire.

Fuses have current **ratings**, which specify the maximum current they will allow through them. If a current exceeds the number of amps specified, the wire inside the fuse melts and cuts off the electricity supply. The fuse is said to have 'blown'.

It is possible to calculate the fuse rating required to protect an appliance. For example, the current required by a 2,400 watt electric fire supplied with 240

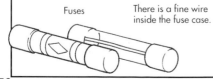

Fuses

There is a fine wire inside the fuse case.

volts, is calculated as follows:

Current $(\mathbf{I}) = \dfrac{\text{power rating } (\mathbf{P})}{\text{voltage } (\mathbf{V})}$

$= \dfrac{2400}{240}$

$= 10$ amps maximum

A 13 A fuse should be used in the kettle.

The cable bringing electricity into a house contains three wires, the **live**, the **neutral** and the **earth** wire. The live and neutral wires carry the current. The earth wire is a safety device. It provides a very low resistance path between the casing of an appliance and ground through which an electric current can escape into the Earth. This reduces the danger of electric shocks which may occur if the insulation around the wires inside an appliance or a plug becomes worn and the live wire touches the casing. The electricity supply may then begin to flow through the casing and through anybody touching the appliance.

*Generator, 61; Nuclear fission, 44; Alternating current, 40; Transformers, 41; Voltage, 32.

# Household electrical circuits

Electricity is carried around a house by **circuits**. There are three main types of circuit: **ring mains**, **lighting circuits** and the **cooker circuit**. Appliances are arranged in these circuits in *parallel\**. This ensures that if one appliance breaks or is switched off the others in the circuit still function.

The electricity cable enters the house through a **fuse box** containing a fuse which limits the current in the cable. It also contains fuses to protect each of the electrical circuits in the house. Fuses and switches used in the circuits are placed in the live wire of an electricity cable. This means that if a fuse blows or a switch is turned off, the current does not continue to flow. The appliances are connected into the circuit by three-pin or two-pin plugs as shown below.

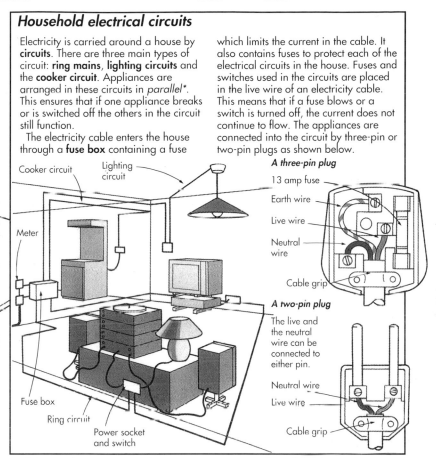

Cooker circuit

Lighting circuit

Meter

Fuse box

Ring circuit

Power socket and switch

*A three-pin plug*

13 amp fuse

Earth wire

Live wire

Neutral wire

Cable grip

*A two-pin plug*

The live and the neutral wire can be connected to either pin.

Neutral wire

Live wire

Cable grip

# Electrical energy and power

The amount of **electrical energy** converted by an appliance into other forms such as heat or light is calculated with the following equation:

**Energy (E) = p.d. (V) × current (I) × time (t)**
(in joules)  (in volts)  (in amps)  (in seconds)

**Electrical power** is the rate at which electrical energy is converted. Power is calculated with the following equation:

**Power (P) = $\dfrac{\text{energy (V × I × t)}}{\text{time (t)}}$ = V × I**
(in watts)  (in joules/in seconds)

Electrical power is measured in watts (W). Larger quantities of power are measured in kilowatts (1,000 watts).

# Paying for electricity

As an electricity cable enters a house it passes through a meter box. The meter measures how much electrical energy a household uses in **kilowatt-hours** (**kW hr**). One kilowatt-hour is the amount of electrical energy used by a 1 k W device in one hour and is called one **unit**. The amount of energy an appliance uses depends on its power rating and the time for which it is used. It is calculated using the following equation:

**Energy used = power (P) × time (t)**
(in units)    (in kW)  (in hours)

For example, an appliance rated at 5 kW, used for 2 hours, uses 10 units of energy.

# Energy, power and the environment

Energy is needed to generate the electrical energy that provides light, heat and transport all over the world. Careful management of fuel resources and investment in new technology will ensure we have enough energy in the future.

## Comparing energy sources

The different sources of energy used worldwide have different benefits and costs. Some resources produce more energy than others, some are expensive to exploit and others are difficult to transport. Economic and political considerations usually determine why governments and companies chose a particular source of energy. However, as evidence of the damaging effects of pollution increases, environmental issues are becoming more and more important.

## Hydro-electricity

More than 20% of the world's power comes from **hydro-electricity**. The water that is held high up in the lakes behind hydro-electric dams has 'stored' *potential energy** and is at high pressure. It is used to drive *turbines**, which produce electricity in *generators**. Although the initial building costs are high, the dams go on to provide a limitless supply of electricity at little cost. Hydro-electric power produces no waste or pollution.

Building the large dams, however, can cause political, social and environmental problems. Often when dams are constructed large areas of fertile land must be cleared of people and animals before flooding. 'Water wars' may develop when dams are built on rivers which run through several countries. For example, if Turkey built a dam across the River Euphrates, downstream the people of Syria would have no river water while the lake behind the dam filled up. The Iraqis, even further downstream, would also be deprived of water.

The lakes behind dams can become blocked by silt (soil carried by rivers). For example, the Sanmenxia Dam on the Huang Ho River in China, built in 1960, was taken out of action after just four years when its lake filled with silt. In hot countries the lakes can cause an increase in diseases, such as bilharzia, caused by tiny organisms in still water.

## Nuclear power

Almost 20% of the world's electricity is provided by nuclear power. Initially it seemed cheap. Vast amounts of energy can be produced from small amounts of fuel. For example, two pellets of nuclear fuel the size of sugar lumps can produce the same amount of energy as two and a half tonnes of coal.

Today, however, many countries are cutting back on nuclear power. Although experts predicted the huge cost of building nuclear power stations, they failed to consider the massive cost of research, of incorporating rigorous safety features, and of reprocessing the nuclear waste produced by the power stations.

Public fears about nuclear power have been aroused by nuclear catastrophes such as those at 'Three Mile Island' in the USA and Chernobyl in USSR. On a smaller scale, the increased number of cases of leukaemia (cancer of the blood), in people working in and living near nuclear power stations, has caused concern.

This sign warns of the presence of radioactive substances.

*Potential energy, 13; Turbines, Generators, 61.

## Oil

**Oil** and **natural gas**, which are *fossil fuels\**, provide over 60% of the world's energy requirements. They can be stored and transported easily and, at present, resources are plentiful. However, if energy consumption continues at its current rate, in 20 to 40 years new reserves will be increasingly difficult to locate and extract.

The price and availability of oil is controlled by the oil producing countries in the Middle East. This can cause problems for other countries which become dependent on imported fuel. For example, in 1976 the USA suffered from its dependency on imported oil when prices increased by 400%.

The burning of oil and gas contributes to major environmental problems such as the *greenhouse effect\** and acid rain (see below). Oil accidentally spilled on land is messy, poisonous and a fire hazard. It can make soil intertile for

More areas undersea are drilled for oil as resources on land are being used up.

many years. At sea, oil spilled from tankers or oil rigs can kill sea birds and fish, destroying the livelihoods of fishermen. In March 1989 an oil tanker called the Exxon Valdez caused a slick of up to 2,400 square kilometres. Experts predict the damage could take over ten years to clear up. Oil companies are often unwilling to spend the money and time necessary to repair the damage oil spillage inflicts on the environment.

## Acid rain

**Acid rain** is a damaging mixture of rain or snow with polluting chemicals, such as sulphuric acid and nitric acid, which are produced by the burning of fossil fuels. The acid can kill trees, people and animals, pollute soil and damage the outside of buildings.

Acid rain can now be prevented by the installation of new anti-pollution technology in power stations. However, many countries say they cannot afford the expensive equipment needed.

## Energy efficiency

As the world population increases and third world countries develop, the demand for energy will increase. Knowledge and technology must be shared between developed countries and the third world, to enable the third world to develop their own efficient and appropriate ways of producing energy.

Greater energy conservation and efficiency is needed in order not to use up the world's energy resources. More money must be provided for research into cleaner, safer, renewable energy sources. Examples of these are solar power, wind power, wave power, tidal power, geothermal power and the burning of biomass (the energy stored in living or dead plant and animal matter,

such as wood and dung).

Money must be invested to develop appliances which require less energy to function. For example, light bulbs have been developed recently which use less than half the amount of electricity used by standard light bulbs. Refrigerators are being produced which use only a fifth of the electricity used by other refrigerators of the same size.

A collection of wind generators on a 'wind farm' in Altamont Pass, California

*Fossil fuels, 14; Greenhouse effect, 29.

53

# Circuit symbols and number notation

This table shows the main symbols used to represent the various components used in electric circuits.

There are many more circuit symbols, but the table includes all the components that appear in this book.

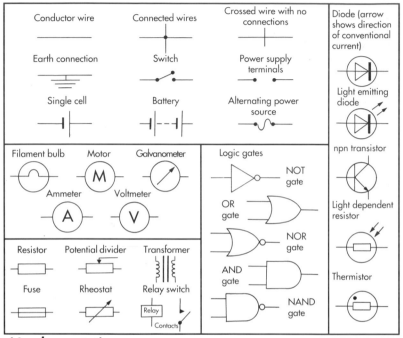

## Number notation

Very large or very small numbers (e.g. 10,000,000 or 0.000001) take a long time to write out and are difficult to read. For this reason a method called **index notation** is used instead. This notation indicates the position of the decimal point in a number by showing what power of ten the number should be raised to.

| | |
|---|---|
| 1,000,000 | is written $10^6$ |
| 100,000 | is written $10^5$ |
| 10,000 | is written $10^4$ |
| 1,000 | is written $10^3$ |
| 100 | is written $10^2$ |
| 10 | is written $10^1$ |
| 1 | is written $10^0$ |
| 0.1 | is written $10^{-1}$ |
| 0.01 | is written $10^{-2}$ |
| 0.001 | is written $10^{-3}$ |
| 0.0001 | is written $10^{-4}$ |
| 0.00001 | is written $10^{-5}$ |
| 0.000001 | is written $10^{-6}$ |

If you have a large or small number, move the decimal point until it is after the first numeral. Write 10 to the power of the number of places you have moved the decimal point. If you move the decimal point to the left the index is positive, e.g. $10^9$. If you move the point to the right the index is negative, e.g. $10^{-2}$.

For example:

| | |
|---|---|
| 32,874 | is written $3.2874 \times 10^4$ |
| 3,000 | is written $3 \times 10^3$ |
| 45.7 | is written $4.57 \times 10^1$ |
| 0.98 | is written $9.8 \times 10^{-1}$ |
| 0.00287 | is written $2.87 \times 10^{-3}$ |

When multiplying numbers, their indices are added together. For example:
$$10^6 \times 10^{-4} = 10^2.$$

When dividing one number by another, the indices are subtracted as follows :
$$10^8 \div 10^5 = 10^3$$

# Graphs

A **graph** is a visual representation of how one quantity changes in relation to another. Graphs can be used to show the information gained from an experiment.

## Constructing a graph

1. Draw two axes. Along the **x-axis** plot the quantity which is varied during an experiment. This is called the **independent variable**. Along the **y-axis** plot the quantity which changes as a result. This is called the **dependent variable**.

Label each axis with the quantity which is plotted along it and the quantity's unit, e.g. distance (m) or time (s).

2. Mark the **scale** of each quantity along its axis. (The scales do not have to be the same on both axes.) When choosing scales, use the squares on your graph paper to represent values which make plotting the points easy (e.g. avoid the squares representing multiples of three).

3. Plot the points on your graph, marking each one with a cross **X** or a dot within a circle ⊙.

Draw a smooth curve or straight line which best fits the points. This is called the **line of best fit**. The points may be scattered about this line. One or two may be a long way from the line due to experimental error.

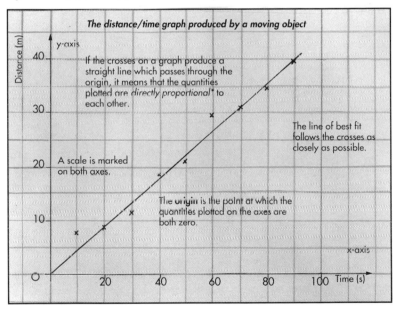

The distance/time graph produced by a moving object

y-axis

If the crosses on a graph produce a straight line which passes through the origin, it means that the quantities plotted are *directly proportional** to each other.

The line of best fit follows the crosses as closely as possible.

A scale is marked on both axes.

The origin is the point at which the quantities plotted on the axes are both zero.

x-axis

## Calculating the gradient of a graph

The **gradient** shows the rate of change of the quantity plotted on the y-axis with that plotted on the x-axis. The gradient of a straight line graph is value Δ y divided by Δ x (where Δ means 'change in').

The unit of the gradient is the unit of the quantity y/x. For example, the unit of the gradient of the graph shown here is m/s (distance/time).

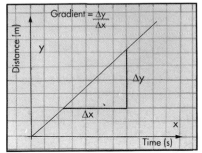

Gradient = $\frac{\Delta y}{\Delta x}$

*Directly proportional, 61.

# Sample questions and answers

This section contains some of the more difficult mathematical ideas used in physics. It includes examples of how to use some of the equations which appear in the coloured section of this book, and some new and more complex equations are introduced. There are sample examination questions and model answers to show you how to tackle certain types of question.

The mathematical ideas and examples appear under the heading of the topic to which they relate. The page number which follows each heading indicates where you can find the topic in this book.

## Pressure (page 9)

The pressure at a certain depth in a fluid can be calculated with the following equation:
**Pressure in a fluid (P)**
= **depth of liquid (h) x density of fluid (d) x acceleration due to gravity (g)**

This equation can only be used when the density throughout the fluid is constant.

**Example A** : What is the pressure due to the water at the bottom of a lake which is 20 m deep. (The density of the water is 1,000 kg/m³.)
**Answer A** : P = hdg
= 20 x 1,000 x 9.81
= **1.96 x 10⁵ N/m²**

In the atmosphere the density of air is not constant with height. A *mercury barometer** can be used to measure atmospheric pressure.

**Example B** : What is the value of the atmospheric pressure which supports a column of mercury of height 76 cm (76 cm = 0.76 m) in a mercury barometer. (The density of mercury is 13,600 kg/m³.)

**Answer B** : P = hdg
= 0.76 x 13,600 x 9.81
= 101,000
= **1.01 x 10⁵ N/m²**
To calculate the total pressure at the bottom of a 20 m deep lake, the atmospheric pressure and the pressure of

the water must be added together.
Pressure = 1.01 x 10⁵ + 1.96 x 10⁵
= **2.97 x 10⁵ N/m²**

## Linear motion (page 10)

The following equations relate to moving objects:
**Average velocity = change in *displacement** (d)**
                    **time taken (t)**
and
**Acceleration (a) = change in velocity (v-u)**
                   **time taken for change (t)**
(where v is the final velocity and u is the original velocity).

These equations are usually used on their own, but occasionally you may need to use them together, as shown in the example below.

**Example C** : Calculate the value of acceleration due to gravity using the following results gained from the experiment described on page 11. A steel ball falls a distance of 1 m in 0.45 s.

**Answer C** : If the steel ball's initial velocity (u) is 0, and its final velocity is v, its average velocity $= \dfrac{v}{2} = \dfrac{d}{t}$
this can be rearranged as $v = \dfrac{2d}{t}$
If its acceleration $(a) = \dfrac{v - u}{t} = \dfrac{v}{t}$
then, $a = \dfrac{2d}{t^2}$
$= \dfrac{2 \times 1}{0.45^2}$
= **9.9 m/s²**

## Velocity/time graphs (page 11)

The velocity/time graph produced by a moving object can be used to calculate the object's acceleration and the distance it travels in a given time.

**Example D** : A car accelerates uniformly from rest to a velocity of 20 m/s in 15 s. It then travels at constant velocity for 20 s before decelerating uniformly to rest in 10 s.
From the following velocity/time graph below calculate a) the object's acceleration, b) its deceleration and c) the total distance it has travelled.

*Mercury barometer, 9; Displacement, 61.

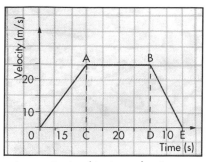

**Answer D** : An object's acceleration or deceleration is equal to the gradient of the velocity/time graph it produces.

a) Acceleration $= \dfrac{AC}{OC} = \dfrac{20}{15}$

$= \textbf{1.33 m/s}^2$

b) Deceleration $= \dfrac{BD}{DE} = \dfrac{20}{10}$

$= \textbf{2 m/s}^2$

c) The distance travelled by the object is equal to the area under the velocity/time graph. This is calculated as follows:
Distance = area OAC + area ABDC + area BED
$= (\frac{1}{2} \times 15 \times 20) + (20 \times 20) + (\frac{1}{2} \times 10 \times 20)$
$= 150 + 400 + 100$
$= \textbf{650 m}$

## Momentum (page 12)

According to the principle of the conservation of momentum, when objects collide, their total momentum is the same before and after the collision (as long as no outside forces act). For two objects in collision, this principle can be written:

**Momentum before = momentum after**

$$m_1u_1 + m_2u_2 = m_1v_1 + m_2v_2$$

(where $m_1$ and $m_2$ are the masses of two objects, $u_1$ and $u_2$ are their velocities before impact and $v_1$ and $v_2$ to their velocities after impact).

**Example E** : A car of mass 2,000 kg, moving at 3 m/s, collides with a stationary car of mass 1,000 kg. After the impact they move together. Calculate the final velocity of the cars after the impact.

**Answer E** : From the principle of conservation of momentum:

$$m_1u_1 + m_2u_2 = (m_1+m_2) \times v$$
$$(2,000 \times 3) + 0 = (2,000 + 1,000) \times v$$
$$6,000 = 3,000v$$
$$v = \textbf{2 m/s}$$

The principle of conservation of momentum applies to all interactions, including explosions (as long as no external forces act). This is demonstrated in the following example.

**Example F** : A bullet of mass 0.01 kg is fired from a rifle of mass 4 kg. If the rifle recoils with a velocity of 2.5 m/s, find the velocity of the bullet.

**Answer F** : The total momentum of the rifle and bullet before the explosion is zero. Therefore, the total momentum afterwards is zero too. The velocity of the rifle must be considered to be a negative quantity as it is moving in the opposite direction to the bullet.

$$0 = (0.01 \times v_1) - (4 \times 2.5)$$
$$0.01 \times v_1 = 10$$
$$v_1 = \textbf{1,000 m/s}$$

## The expansion of gases (page 27)

When considering the expansion of a fixed mass of gas, three quantities must be considered: pressure, temperature and volume. If any of these quantities changes, it is possible to work out how the other quantities are affected by the change using the following equation which is called the **general gas equation**:

$$\frac{p_1V_1}{T_1} = \frac{p_2V_2}{T_2}$$

(where $p_1$, $V_1$ and $T_1$, refer to the pressure, volume and temperature in kelvins of a gas before it undergoes a change, and $p_2$, $V_2$ and $T_2$ to the values afterwards).

It is important to remember that the temperature must always be in kelvins. The pressure of a gas is often measured in **atmospheres**. One atmosphere is the pressure considered to be normal atmospheric pressure. A pressure of one atmosphere would support a mercury column of height 76cm.

The general gas equation can often be simplified. For example, if the temperature of a gas remains constant ($T_1 = T_2$), then, $p_1V_1 = p_2V_2$

If its volume remains constant ($V_1 = V_2$), then, $\dfrac{p_1}{T_1} = \dfrac{p_2}{T_2}$

If its pressure remains constant ($p_1 = p_2$), then, $\dfrac{V_1}{T_1} = \dfrac{V_2}{T_2}$

**Example G** : If $2m^3$ of a gas at 1 atmosphere pressure is compressed to $0.25m^3$ at constant temperature, what is its new pressure?

**Answer G** : As temperature is constant, then, $p_1V_1 = p_2V_2$

$1 \times 2 = p_2 \times 0.25$

$p_2 =$ **8 atmospheres**

**Example H** : A gas at 27 °C (300 K) is heated at constant pressure until its volume has doubled. What is the new temperature of the gas?

**Answer H** : As pressure is constant, then, $\dfrac{V_1}{T_1} = \dfrac{V_2}{T_2}$

$\dfrac{V_1}{300} = \dfrac{2 \times V_1}{T_2}$

$T_2 = 2 \times 300$

$=$ **600 K (327 °C)**

## Ohm's law (page 34-35)

Ohm's law produces the equation:

**Resistance (R) = $\dfrac{\text{p.d. (V)}}{\text{current (I)}}$**

This relationship can apply to single components or any group of components in an electrical circuit.

**Example I** : For the circuit below, calculate: a) the current through each of the resistors in the circuit, and b) the total current flowing.

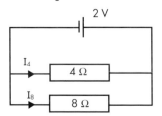

**Answer I** : a) The resistors are in parallel, therefore, the p.d. across each resistor is 2 V.

If Ohm's law is applied to the 4 Ω resistor, then $I_4 = \dfrac{V}{R}$

$= \dfrac{2}{4}$

$=$ **0.5 amps**

If Ohm's law is applied to the 8 Ω resistor, then $I_8 = \dfrac{2}{8}$

$=$ **0.25 amps**

b) Total current $= I_4 + I_8$

$= 0.5 + 0.25$

$=$ **0.75 amps**

**Example J** : For the circuit below calculate: a) the current flowing, and b) the p.d. across each of the resistors.

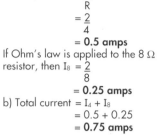

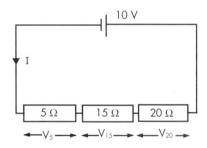

**Answer J** :

a) Total resistance $= 5 + 15 + 20$

$= 40 \; \Omega$

If Ohm's law is applied to the whole circuit, then $I = \dfrac{V}{R} = \dfrac{10}{40}$

$=$ **0.25 amps**

b) If Ohm's law is applied to each of the resistors in turn, then:

P.d. across 5 Ω resistor ($V_5$) $= 0.25 \times 5$

$=$ **1.25 V**

P.d. across 15 Ω resistor ($V_{15}$) $= 0.25 \times 15$

$=$ **3.75 V**

P.d. across 20 Ω resistor ($V_{20}$) $= 0.25 \times 20$

$=$ **5 V**

**Example K**: Calculate the current through each of the three resistors in the following circuit diagram.

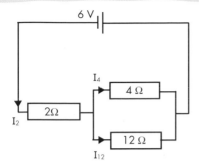

**Answer K** : The combined resistance of the 4 Ω and 12 Ω resistor in parallel is calculated as follows:

$$\frac{1}{R} = \frac{1}{4} + \frac{1}{12}$$

$$= \frac{3 + 1}{12}$$

$$= \frac{4}{12}$$

$$\frac{1}{R} = \frac{1}{3}$$

$$R = 3 \ \Omega$$

The total resistance in the circuit (R)

$$R = 2 + 3 = 5 \ \Omega$$

If Ohm's law is applied to the whole circuit, then the total current through the circuit $I_2 = \frac{6}{5}$

$$= 1.2 \ amps$$

If Ohm's law is applied to the 2 Ω resistor, the p.d. across it is:

P.d. $= 1.2 \times 2$

$$= 2.4 \ V$$

Therefore, the p.d. across the 4 Ω and 12 Ω resistors $= 6 - 2.4$

$$= 3.6 \ V$$

If Ohm's law is applied to the 4 Ω resistor and 12 Ω resistor in turn then, the current through the 4 Ω resistor is calculated as follows:

$$I_4 = \frac{3.6}{4}$$

$$= 0.9 \ amps$$

and the current through 12 Ω resistor,

$$I_{12} = \frac{3.6}{12}$$

$$= 0.3 \ amps$$

(Note: $I_2 = I_4 + I_{12}$)

## Transformers (page 41)

The turns ratio shows the relationship between the number of turns of conductor wire on the primary and secondary coils of a transformer and the p.d.s produced in both coils.

**No. primary turns ($N_p$)** = **primary p.d. ($V_p$)**
**No. secondary turns ($N_s$)**    **secondary p.d. ($V_s$)**

**Example L** : If an alternating p.d. of 240 V is applied to the primary coil of a transformer which has 200 turns of wire, what will be the p.d. produced in the secondary coil which has 10 turns?

**Answer L** : $\frac{N_p}{N_s} = \frac{V_p}{V_s}$

$$\frac{200}{10} = \frac{240}{V_s}$$

$$20 = \frac{240}{V_s}$$

$$20 \times V_s = 240$$

$$V_s = \frac{240}{20}$$

$$= 12 \ V$$

Electrical power is calculated with the equation:

$$P = VI$$

(where P is power, V is voltage and I is current).

In a perfectly efficient transformer the electrical power supplied by the primary coil would be equal to the power delivered to the secondary coil. This relationship can be written as follows:

$$V_p \ I_p = V_s \ I_s$$

(where $I_p$ and $I_s$ are the currents in the primary and secondary coils).

**Example M** : Using the same transformer as in example L, calculate the current in the secondary coil ($I_s$) if the current in the primary coil ($I_p$) is 0.1 amp.

**Answer M** : $240 \times 0.1 = 12 \times I_s$

$$24 = 12 \times I_s$$

$$I_s = \frac{24}{12}$$

$$= 2 \ amps$$

# Summary of equations

The following table as acts a summary of some of the important equations in this book. The table contains **derived quantities** which are worked out by dividing or multiplying two or more other quantities. The unit of a derived quantity (called a **derived unit**) is found from its defining equation. Some derived units are given special names. These are shown in the table.

| Derived quantity | Symbol | Defining equation | Derived unit | Name of unit | Abbreviation |
|---|---|---|---|---|---|
| Density | d | $d = \dfrac{\text{mass}}{\text{volume}}$ | $kg/m^3$ | | |
| Moment | | Moment = force × perpendicular distance | $N\,m$ | Newton metre | $N\,m$ |
| Pressure | P | $P = \dfrac{\text{force}}{\text{area}}$ | $N/m^2$ | Pascal | $Pa$ |
| Velocity | v | $v = \dfrac{\text{distance moved}}{\text{time}}$ | $m/s$ | | |
| Acceleration | a | $a = \dfrac{\text{change in velocity}}{\text{time}}$ | $m/s^2$ | | |
| Force | F | F = mass × acceleration | $kg\,m/s^2$ | Newton | $N$ |
| Momentum | | Momentum = mass × velocity | $kg\,m/s$ | | |
| Energy | E | Capacity to do work | $Nm$ | Joule | $J$ |
| Work | W | W = force × distance | $Nm$ | Joule | $J$ |
| Power | P | $P = \dfrac{\text{work done}}{\text{time}}$ | $J/s$ | Watt | $W$ |
| Frequency | f | Number of waves per second | $1/s$ | Hertz | $Hz$ |
| Electric charge | Q | Q = current × time | $A\,s$ | Coulomb | $C$ |
| Potential difference | V | $V = \dfrac{\text{energy transferred}}{\text{charge}}$ | $J/C$ | Volt | $V$ |
| Resistance | R | $R = \dfrac{\text{potential difference}}{\text{current}}$ | $V/A$ | Ohm | $\Omega$ |

# *Glossary*

The glossary explains some of the more difficult terms used in this book. The terms defined appear in **bold**, as do other related words which are used in the definition. Words within the explanations which have their own entries in this list are followed by a †.

**Directly proportional**. When applied to two quantities, if one quantity changes by a certain proportion, then the other changes by the same proportion. For example, if one quantity is doubled, the other quantity is doubled too.

**Displacement**. A measurement of the distance and direction of an object at any time from a chosen fixed point. Displacement is a *vector** quantity.

**Earth potential**. The *electrical potential** of the planet Earth. The Earth is able to supply or absorb electrical charge without changing its own potential. It is considered to be at zero electrical potential.

**Element**. A substance which cannot be split into simpler substances by a chemical reaction. Atoms of the same element have the same number of protons in their nucleus. There are over one hundred known elements.

**Generator**. A machine which converts kinetic energy into electrical energy. The kinetic energy may be provided by an engine or a turbine†.The *simple dynamo** is an example of a generator.

**Inversely proportional**. When applied to two quantities, this means that one quantity is directly proportional† to the reciprocal† of the other. For example, if one quantity is doubled, the other quantity is halved.

**Medium**. The substance or space in which objects exist and phenomena take place. For example, glass is described as a medium when light travels through it.

**Ozone layer**. A layer of gas which forms part of the Earth's upper atmosphere. It absorbs some of the harmful ultra-violet radiation from the Sun.

The ozone layer is being destroyed by man-made chemicals. If the ozone layer continues to be destroyed and more UV radiation is allowed to reach the Earth, it may lead to an increase in the number of cases of skin cancer and be harmful to crop production.

**Rate**. The amount by which one quantity changes in relation to another. For example, acceleration is the rate of change of velocity in relation to time. (Note that the second quantity is not time in all cases.)

**Reactor**. The container in a nuclear power plant in which atoms are split to release a vast amount of energy.

**Reciprocal**. The value obtained from a number when one is divided by that number. The reciprocal of any number x would be $1/x$. For example, the reciprocal of 10 is $1/10$ which is 0.1).

**Spectrum**. A particular range of wavelengths or frequencies. For example, the wavelength of the waves which make up the visible spectrum of light range from $4 \times 10^{-7}$ m to $7.5 \times 10^{-7}$ m.

**Turbine**. A device with rotating blades. The blades are turned by a force. For example, jets of steam turn the turbines in a coal-fired power station. The kinetic energy of a moving turbine can be converted into electricity in a generator†.

*A turbine*

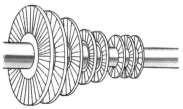

**Vacuum**. A space which is completely empty of matter. A **partial vacuum** is created in a container from which some air or gas has been removed, so that the pressure inside the container is much less than the atmospheric pressure outside it.

**Vaporization**. The change of state from liquid to **vapour**. A liquid will **vaporize** at a temperature called its **boiling point**.

# Index

First published in 1991 by Usborne Publishing
Ltd, 83-85 Saffron Hill, London EC1N 8RT,
England.

The name Usborne and the device 🐝 are
trade marks of Usborne Publishing Ltd.
Printed in Spain.

UE